The Closet Case

ALSO BY TAWANNA SULLIVAN

The Next Girl & Other Lesbian Tales

The

Closet

Case

A Girl Trouble Mystery

TAWANNA SULLIVAN

Published by tpsulli publications
PO Box 15212, Jersey City, NJ 07305
Cover Design by James, GoOnWrite.com

ISBN-13: 978-0-9984327-4-8

Dedicated to Marie Peet, who always let me be myself.

Chapter 1

Gina kicked off her slippers and collapsed into the recliner. "I need a handyman," she said.

"Don't say that too loud," Debra said as she paused the movie. "That dude up the street would definitely volunteer."

Shifting her position on the sofa, Shanice stretched and stifled a yawn. "David? He's still asking you out on the sly?"

The thought made Gina shiver. The day she moved in, David had nearly gotten hit by a car as he raced across the street to help unpack her van. He admitted to living with his parents but spent the rest of the day bragging about his residency at Johns Hopkins. For several weeks afterward, he materialized whenever Gina stepped outside, always offering an invitation to get to know him better.

"You two ran him off," Gina said. She looked at Debra. "David couldn't take your buzz cut and leather boots. He stopped talking to me altogether when Shanice got here. Now he's trying to seduce Ms. Thompson's granddaughter."

"He stills glares at me and puffs out his chest," Debra said. "What do you need a handyman for? I thought Childress was taking care of the basement."

"She is, but this old house has a lot of problems. It's not falling apart, because Aunt Mavis did her best to keep it up, but continued maintenance is important." Gina's bracelets jangled as she began counting off what needed to be done. "Re-grout the bathrooms, replace light fixtures, paint the bedrooms – that's only the beginning."

Debra put down the remote and sat up. "What do you need a man for when you have two able-bodied housemates

1

around? I'm pretty good with my hands." The other women burst into laughter. "What?" Debra asked.

"Remember when you tried to change the light bulb on the porch?" Shanice asked. "You nearly fell into the neighbors' bushes."

"That bumblebee tried to attack me." Debra's admission didn't stem the tide of laughter.

In an effort to compose herself, Shanice gazed around the room. The furniture was outdated but in impeccable shape. There had been no children to scuff up the hardwood floors or damage the walls. Like the other row houses on the block, it had columns on the front porch and other details that gave it a classic look. It felt like a palace after her four years in a dorm. Suddenly, Shanice felt grateful. "Debra is right. We should help out beyond dusting."

Gina agreed. "I have a whole list of chores for you two to tackle."

Cleaning up the backyard would not be an easy one-afternoon task. The neighbors had paved over their grass and turned the lawns into partial basketball courts or parking spaces, but Gina had never wanted to look out from her kitchen window and see a slab of concrete. She envisioned a vegetable garden and parties under star-filled skies.

Debra could feel the dew from the grass soaking through her socks. The droplets made it hard to get a solid hold on the weeds lined along the fence. After several tugs, she got a handful of leaves; the stalk, stripped bare, stood firmly rooted in the earth. Cursing under her breath, Debra threw the leaves into a bag that Shanice held out to her. Beads of sweat ran down her bald head and drenched her eyebrows. "Why am I the one doing the hard work?"

Shanice tried to shield her eyes from the sun. "You're the one who's good with her hands." She leaned against the rusted pole that held up one end of the clothesline. "What are you complaining about? I'm the one who has to clean out the grill."

Her legs started to cramp; Debra stood up and flexed her calves. "You coming out to Clara's with us tonight? Punch drinks are half off on Fruity Friday."

"No," Shanice said. "Don't feel like hanging around a lot of people tonight. Be nice to have the house to myself for a while."

"You're here all day by yourself."

"You act like I don't work during the day."

"I didn't say that, but come on. Working at home does have its advantages." Debra leaned against the fence. "You didn't want to hang out last weekend either. What's up?"

"I can't really afford to do a lot of extra stuff right now."

"A client stiff you? Don't worry about it; drinks are on me."

"It's deeper than that. My client base is drying up."

"Why didn't you say something? Gina and I could —"

"Gina doesn't need to know. I'm okay for a few months."

"You should have billed Renee for that website you created for her."

Shanice bristled at the mention of her ex-girlfriend. "That was a labor of love."

"You can always go corporate."

"Working for someone else is the last thing I want to do. I thought being an independent web developer would give me the flexibility to turn people down, but the only people interested in hiring me are the ones I don't really want to work with. Yesterday, I got a message from a minister who wants a site for his church."

Debra resumed her weed-clutching position, but her knees ached in protest. It had been years since she had been on the high school basketball team, but her joints still hadn't forgiven her. "Let's take a break from this," she said. They walked toward the grill. "Do it. Maybe church websites can be your niche." Shanice rolled her eyes. "I'm serious. It's not unusual for people to fall into their careers. I'm not the deli manager at Chopin Cart because I have a passion for overpriced cheese."

Shanice sighed. Even if she wanted to, she couldn't go to an interview. A month after her cousin's wedding, smoke and baby vomit still soiled the blue pantsuit she wore on professional and formal occasions. She'd never gotten around to having it dry cleaned. "Maybe I'll go into landscaping."

Rusted hinges threatened to break when Shanice pried open the grill. Something moved under the mound of ashes and both women jumped back. The lid fell shut and a scratching sound echoed from the lower chamber.

"We should trim the rosebush," Debra said.

Shanice knocked on the doorframe and Gina looked up from folding laundry. "Come in." She patted a space next to her on the bed. "You don't have to knock when the door is open."

A breeze drifted through the open window. "My dad said never go into a woman's bedroom unless you've been invited. He was talking to my brother, but it's good advice."

Gina hid a blush behind a smile. "Finished with the yard for today?"

"No, I wanted to tell you something." Shanice hesitated. "The grill can't be saved and...I need to borrow a dress."

Chapter 2

Shanice felt self-conscious when she turned in to the parking lot. Her gray Dodge was an ancient relic compared to the luxury vehicles she pulled next to. Hauling her briefcase from the backseat, she took in the monstrous building in front of her.

The Montgomery Cove Condominium complex housed forty-two deluxe units with high ceilings and spectacular views of the bay. Twenty years ago, it was one of several abandoned warehouses on a rat-infested pier. A combination of federal grants, tax incentives, refurbished storefronts, and inflated price tags had transformed the area into real estate gold.

It was the ideal place for her prospective client, Pastor Walter Robinson of Hope Reborn Baptist Church. The Cove put him two buses and a light rail transfer away from Griffin Hill, the lower-middle class neighborhood that housed his congregation. But this was the last place she wanted to be at eight o'clock on a Saturday morning.

Shanice had started making websites in high school. As a college sophomore, it became an easy way to earn extra money. Back then, she could dazzle the HTML-challenged with a script that changed background colors with the click of a mouse. Now the most basic web-hosting packages came with pre-installed website templates and anyone with the ability to drag and drop could have a site running in minutes. While she juggled classes and relationship drama, her web-designing skills were rendered virtually irrelevant.

There had been a lot of women. Passionate and

indiscriminate, she fell in and out of love every few months.

A brand-new college graduate, Shanice had sworn off sex for the third time when Renee accidentally bumped into her at a café. It took two months of direct messaging and flirtatious phone calls before she accepted the closeted singer's invitation to coffee.

An independent career-minded woman who had a firm grasp on what she wanted, Renee was nothing like her exes. Shanice declared herself ready for a real one-on-one committed relationship.

It was doomed from the start. Renee was deep in the closet. The few times that they did appear together in public, she was terrified Shanice would accidentally out her. What would it look like if the up-and-coming gospel singer the *Edmondson Enquirer* dubbed "the Tramaine Hawkins of a new generation" went to the movies with a dyke?

That was why Shanice's stomach did a little quake when Pastor Robinson revealed that Renee had recommended her. What a joke. Here she was in new stockings and a borrowed skirt, trying desperately to look like the sweet young lady her ex had wanted her to transform into. Shoved into three-inch pointed-toe heels, her aching feet could barely navigate the cobblestone walkway.

Shanice willed herself to move past discomfort. She needed to concentrate on the present, on convincing the pastor that she could produce a site better than whoever had created their travesty of a Myspace page.

In preparation for the meeting, she had watched a few episodes of their public access cable show – a badly lit video of their Sunday service. Pastor Robinson's sermons started off like academic lectures, but then he would pounce on the theme. The transformation started with a loosening of his collar. As he rocked back and forth, his tongue broke free from the classroom and words skipped out in a familiar rhythm. Oliver the organist, a man with a pompadour, could always be counted on for a hearty "Amen."

As she walked into the lobby, the guard at the front desk

straightened up and gave her a hundred-watt smile. "Good morning. My name is James and I'll be happy to announce your arrival. Are you here to see the Morgans?"

"The Robinsons."

He snapped his fingers. "That would have been my second guess. Your name, please?"

"Shanice Wilkins."

"Beautiful name. I'm sure there's a beautiful girl hidden somewhere under that frown."

Great, Shanice thought. *I look as bad as I feel.*

A few minutes later, she rang the bell of unit 6E. Pastor Robinson looked older in person. His wrinkles, usually smoothed out by makeup, made his forehead look like the Grand Canyon. He smiled through bloodshot eyes.

"Good morning, Ms. Wilkins. Please come in." When he stepped back, Shanice walked into a wall of Old Spice.

The living room was mostly bare white walls and mahogany bookcases. She tried to get comfortable on the sofa, but the brown leather was cold against her calves. When her eyes set upon the plate of cookies in the middle of the coffee table, her stomach roared. Getting ready for the interview had meant forgoing breakfast. The minister had barely invited her to partake before she had secured an assortment of cookies in a napkin.

A door swung open and a tall woman carrying a tea set entered the room. Her blue floral pantsuit provided a much needed flash of color. When Pastor Robinson introduced her as his wife, Shanice almost dropped her coconut macaroon. Ms. Barbara looked nothing like the stone-faced, floor-length-skirt-wearing woman who read the announcements at Sunday service.

"A church could sprout on every corner, but it still wouldn't be enough to fill the void in humanity's collective soul," Pastor Robinson began. "It's time to expand our outreach to the Internet. Renee said you were a dream to work with and economical."

Shanice smiled. If the minister expected a free website,

he was going to be disappointed. "Renee had a clear vision of what she wanted. That helped reduce the time needed to develop her site."

Ms. Barbara smiled. "She probably had every detail planned out."

It's time to move this conversation forward, Shanice thought. After a few sips of tea, she launched into the usual pitch. "Are you looking to provide static information or include some interactivity? Basic text and images or media files?" She pulled a laptop from her briefcase. "I can show you some websites I've created in the past, but I wouldn't dump your information into a generic template. I design a site according to a client's specific need."

She looked up and was met by two pairs of anxious eyes. Something was wrong. "Is this a bad time?" she asked. "We can reschedule."

Pastor Robinson's cup rattled when he sat it down. "Renee is trying to blackmail us and we want you to stop her."

Gently taking her husband's hand, Ms. Barbara produced a weak smile. "It's not as dramatic as all that, but Renee has played a prank on us that's gone too far."

The discomfort she felt blossomed into a full-blown stomachache. "I don't understand. You aren't interested in a website?"

Pastor Robinson dabbed at the beads of sweat peppering his forehead. They were navigating dangerous waters. "We know you handled a certain matter for Renee involving her sister. We think our situation warrants the same discretion."

Shanice remembered that incident well. If the Robinsons knew about StoneTalker1769, Renee had taken them into her confidence. They probably knew about other things. Still, Shanice resisted the urge to let down her guard and began to pack her bag. "I don't know what your game is, but I don't appreciate being invited here under false pretenses."

"Walter, can you give us a few minutes?" He reluctantly disappeared into the kitchen. Edging closer, Ms. Barbara removed a manila envelope from her purse. "We will pay you for your time. Just hear me out. Renee and I have a history."

Shanice wanted to ask if they had been lovers, but her tongue was paralyzed as her head filled with unholy images.

"I was her mentor," Ms. Barbara continued. "After a few write-ups in the paper, Renee stopped putting in the work to establish herself. She expected me to introduce her to people who would automatically advance her gospel career. One day, I told her the truth: she's no better than any other gifted choir diva. Then it got nasty."

An angry Renee could spit poisoned barbs at your soul. "I've been on the receiving end of a couple of temper tantrums," Shanice said. The memory made her wince.

"Despite our personal feelings, we remained polite in public. So it didn't seem odd when Renee introduced me to Lisa Whitmore at the Black Moses fundraiser. Lisa and I had so much in common that we became fast friends."

Pushing the tray aside, Ms. Barbara took two photos from the envelope and put them on the coffee table. "Lisa and I met for lunch. A few weeks later, Walter and I received this."

The first image showed Ms. Barbara and a beautiful young woman huddled over a plate of pasta. The sly smiles, a hand touching an arm – the two had shared something deeply personal. Looking at the second photo, Shanice's eyes strayed from the couple and saw a waiter in the background. "That's Lisa? Someone with a zoom lens has tried to make it look like you two are alone. Maybe even more than friends."

Ms. Barbara handed her a third picture showing the inside of a hotel room. The bed had been made – the crisp sheets tucked away perfectly. "This is my room. That's my watch on the night table and my luggage in the corner. Now turn it over."

Shanice obliged and found a message scrawled in big black block letters: DON'T YOU THINK IT'S TIME FOR

THE TRUTH TO COME OUT?

"These pictures tell a lie that's preposterous, but no one cares if a salacious story is untrue. When these photos arrived, I immediately called Lisa. Her number had been disconnected."

Pastor Robinson returned, clearly agitated. "Have you asked her yet?"

"Walter, please, I'm getting to it." Sighing, Ms. Barbara continued. "I called Renee demanding answers. She laughed and hung up on me. Later, she called back and left a horrible message. She enjoyed hearing me upset and said I deserved every nasty thing coming to me."

Shanice didn't believe it. "I can't see Renee blackmailing anyone. It's not like she doesn't have her own secrets."

"That's just it," Ms. Barbara said. "There hasn't been an explicit threat. This could be a thoughtless prank or a warning."

Pastor Robinson folded his arms and from his mouth came the voice of a spiritual orator. "We want you to find out what Renee is planning and talk her out of it."

"I haven't spoken to her in months." Shanice got up, determined to leave. "Besides, sounds like it's Lisa you should be looking for. You have no proof that Renee has anything to do with this."

Ms. Barbara quickly gathered the pictures. "Someone else may have held the camera, but she is responsible. She practically admitted to it on the phone."

"I don't know what your friend's game is," Pastor Robinson said, "but keep in mind that threats can have legal consequences." He paused to let the gravity of his words sink in. "If Renee insists on telling lies about my wife, we'll have no other recourse than to tell the truth about her."

Shanice wanted to turn and walk out, but she couldn't move. The Robinsons were misguided but serious. If Renee was in trouble, didn't she at least owe her ex-lover a warning? "I can't make any promises, but I'll talk to her."

Pastor Robinson began to discuss a fee. Barbara turned

away, her soft brown eyes brimming with tears. Shanice tried to ignore the beginning pangs of a headache. *What the hell have I gotten myself into?*

Chapter 3

Weekends in Maynard Wood guaranteed one thing – parking would be scarce. A jeep had wedged itself into the spot Shanice had vacated earlier, which left her no choice but to circle the block. A lot of people were outside enjoying the weather, mowing lawns, chatting with each other, but the cars stayed put. Most of her neighbors were retirees with no place to go during the week and family who visited on the weekend.

For over half a century, Maynard Wood had been a predominately black working- to middle-class neighborhood. During the eighties, the media tried to portray the community as a crime-ridden cesspool on the edge of Armageddon. The mayor declared it a blight on the city of Ardola. In truth, the industrial area next to Maynard saw an increase in crime when the textile factory closed. The owners of the building abandoned it, local officials ignored what went on in its darkened corners, and its decay spread to the community.

In the nineties, the neighborhood changed again. Thanks to the re-routing of the M29 bus line, college students from out of state ventured into the area in search of cheap rentals. Maynard was one of the neighborhoods chosen for the city's Rejuvenate-Reinvigorate Program. A developer bought the old textile building and converted it into condos. Anticipating an influx of new residents, the city finally leveled uprooted sidewalks, fixed broken street lamps, and replaced the rusted-out equipment on the playground.

Real estate agents, sensing opportunity, followed soon

behind. For the most part, they were disappointed. Homeowners who had endured the pain of recession and crime saw no reason to sell now that the city was investing in the neighborhood.

New condo owners, mostly young white professionals, wholeheartedly bought into the idea that – by their very presence – they had resurrected the community. One time, representatives of the condo association reached out to long-time residents in hopes of starting a community watch program. They had only knocked on a few doors before they discovered that a program already existed. Word quickly spread that the newcomers hadn't done their homework.

Occasional challenges in communication aside, old and new residents got along – except for the occasional dust-up over a parking space.

After a third fruitless drive down her street, Shanice gave up and ended up two blocks away next to Archer Elementary School. Thanks to a pair of sneakers in the trunk, she wouldn't have to hobble all the way home. The next challenge would be getting past Jenkins and Adler without being sucked into an endless conversation. Friends and next-door neighbors for over two decades, they sat on their porches to discuss the state of the world and dispense unsolicited advice to passersby.

As Shanice rounded the corner, the elderly gentlemen were teasing a teenager with a lopsided haircut. Squinting, Jenkins leaned forward. "Boy, who did that to you? Hope you got a discount; they only took fifty percent off." He smiled and a gold-capped tooth gleamed in the sunlight.

"It's not an accident," the young man insisted. "It's my style. I don't want to look like everyone else."

Adler laughed. "Some girl done told you that you look good and got you around here looking like a raggedy Gumby."

Shanice quickened her stride but waved as she passed them. "Mornin'," Jenkins called after her. "You lookin' good in that skirt, gal." Once a safe distance, she looked back and saw the young man still trying to make his case.

She got home in time to see a procession of beautiful black women walking out the door. They fluttered around her, some exchanging hugs and air kisses before going on their way. She found Gina and Debra in the dining room clearing away brunch. "I'm back. What did I miss?"

Gina smiled. "The first committee meeting for the lesbian health conference."

"It was a nice turnout," said Debra. "I hope they keep their enthusiasm. People love to throw out ideas but disappear when it's time to do any work."

"Those ladies gave up a Saturday morning for the cause – the work has already started." If it was an overcast day, Debra would complain about the dark clouds while Gina would marvel at their shapes.

"Take Grace," Debra said. "She's the kind of woman who won't even bring napkins to a potluck but will knock you over to fill her plate. She was taking up space on the sofa."

"Give the woman a chance. We'll need a social butterfly like her to charm sponsors." Gina started packing away the leftover cold cuts when she turned to Shanice. "Did you have anything to eat today? I can make you a sandwich."

As if on cue, Shanice's stomach began growling. "A sandwich would be great. I ran out without breakfast and I'm really feeling it now."

Gina set aside the roast beef. "How did it go this morning? Are you going to be coding HTML for the Lord?"

"Let me change first and I'll tell you all about it." Shanice bounded up the steps to her room. The stockings that had a stranglehold on her thighs couldn't come off fast enough. More important than ditching the professional drag, though, she had to figure out how much information to reveal.

Officially, Pastor Robinson had ordered a deluxe design package from her. Unofficially, she was to stop her ex from doing something foolish and, if possible, make sure the pictures were destroyed. He had given her a very healthy personal check; she wouldn't have to worry about rent for a while.

Shanice wished her motive was money rather than genuine concern for Renee. Her friends had let her cry on their shoulders during that breakup. Dare she admit missing the woman who had caused her so many tears? No, the whole truth wouldn't do.

She didn't want to talk about her experience at all, but she couldn't let her housemates think the trip was a bust. It was hard not to be jealous of them. Debra came home smelling like lunchmeat, but she never had to worry about finding customers--and she had health insurance! Gina had inherited the house from her great aunt. Without worries of having to provide a roof over her own head, she freely explored the low-paying-but-spiritually-rewarding world of non-profits. They both appeared to be happy with who they were and what they were doing.

Shanice slipped into her standard, all-purpose outfit – a pair of dark blue jeans and a t-shirt. Feeling like herself again, she reassessed the situation. Sitting back and watching the closet implode around Renee was an option. Petty satisfaction would only last so long – especially if it ruined the singer's career. Shanice sighed. Checking in on Renee was the right thing to do.

She came downstairs to a hot roast beef sandwich slathered in sautéed onions and dripping with cheddar. "Wow, this is great!"

Gina took the seat next to her. "Something tells me you had an ordeal this morning and you needed something substantial to hit the spot."

Debra put a Coke in front of her and sat down with her laptop. "So," she asked, "how did it go?"

"The outfit paid off," Shanice said between gulps of soda. "I'll be building a website for Hope Reborn Baptist Church." She hoped that stuffing her mouth with food would keep the conversation to a minimum.

A shadow of skepticism crossed Gina's brow. "Usually a member of the congregation will do work like that for free. Why are they hiring you?"

Gospel music came blaring from Debra's screen. She immediately turned the volume down and turned it toward them to reveal an ugly web page with broken links. "The volunteer experiment failed."

"The package includes the installation of content management software and custom-designed templates. They'll also get a guided foray into the world of social media. My aim is to give the client the means to be self-sufficient." It wasn't a lie; she did agree to build a unique site template for them. Both she and the minister planned on reporting the financial transaction to the IRS. "This should be fairly easy and an endorsement from the pastor could lead to more work."

Debra stole one of Shanice's pickles. "Gina, why are you giving her the third degree? A job is a job, right?"

"I grew up in Hope Reborn," Gina said. "Pastor Robinson and Ms. Barbara tried to steer me in the right direction. It almost worked. You may hear rumors that the pastor has ulterior motives when he works with young women, but he's not like that."

Shanice tried to imagine the frightened man she met that morning as a Lothario on the prowl. "I didn't get that vibe from him at all. Besides, Ms. Barbara is actually the one I'll be reporting to."

Gina's lips relaxed into a smile and she rubbed the back of Shanice's hand. "Good. I've got to look out for my church folks and Ms. Barbara is a smart woman. Anyway, be careful. I don't want anything to happen to one of my favorite tenants."

Chapter 4

The call to Renee had gone better than Shanice expected. A somber "we need to talk" was all it took to secure an audience with her ex.

Awkward didn't even begin to describe their last conversation. Shanice had been preparing for her weekly pilgrimage to the singer's apartment. Every Friday, Renee invited her over for dinner and a movie. Shanice would show up with dessert in hand. Even though they were supposed to be taking it slow, they always ended up in bed before the movie ended.

On that night, the eve of their sixth-month anniversary, Shanice called from the grocery store to see if Renee wanted cheesecake or ice cream. But her lover didn't want anything – including her. "I need a break," she'd said. "More than a break, actually. I told you I'm not ready for a relationship. This is too much, too fast."

Shanice had stood there in the frozen food section with her hand hovering over rocky road ice cream. She did a quick gut check. The feeling reverberating through her body was relief. For weeks, she felt the burden of secrecy wearing away at her, but she had been willing to ride it out a little longer. It never occurred to her that Renee could be unhappy too. Settling on a pint of mint chocolate chip, she said, "It's okay. I understand."

After several uncomfortable moments, Renee's icy voice pierced the silence. "That's all you have to say?"

"I'm agreeing with you." The call promptly disconnected. By the time she reached the checkout line,

Shanice felt her own temper rising. How did she get blindsided? Suddenly, she felt vulnerable. What right did Renee have to be unhappy? Hadn't she gotten everything she wanted?

As the clerk put the change and receipt in her hand, Shanice promised herself that she wouldn't become one of those desperate exes chasing answers. She needed to push down the pain and lock it away. Being a secret lover was exciting at first, but now she was bored. Why should it bother her that Renee ended it?

Now Shanice brushed off past frustrations and focused on the present. One thing she knew – Lisa was not Renee's girlfriend. A person swinging a purse could do nothing for her ex except share make-up tips. Over-conscious about her image, the singer lived with the curse of desiring lovers she could never appear with in public.

Stepping into the elevator of Renee's apartment building, Shanice got nervous. What was the appropriate way to greet an ex? A hug? A kiss on the cheek? Could she touch her without wanting to caress those familiar curves?

Any hope for a loving reunion disappeared with the scowling stranger who met her at the door. The older black woman had close-cropped hair and eyes that were more tired than angry. Wrapped in a blue satin robe, Renee sauntered out of the bedroom and sat on the arm of the sofa. Shanice took a step back. The staring match ended when the behemoth spoke. "This doesn't look like Sister Imogene to me."

Shanice looked past the obstruction to Renee. "Are you going to invite me in or is this a bad time?"

Renee sighed and walked into the kitchen. "Come in, Shanice. Brandy, run to the store and get me some flour."

Brandy moved aside, but her anger intensified. "I'm not even worth a formal introduction?" Getting no response, she cursed under her breath and slammed the door behind her.

That was Brandy Brandeis, Shanice thought. Everyone

knew Harriet "Brandy" Brandeis, the head mechanic and owner of Brandeis Motors. She did a weekly segment on Sunrise Today where, in blue overalls, she leaned against the fender of a Bentley and answered viewer questions about car maintenance and repair. Debra called the segment "new tips from an old dyke."

The scent of cinnamon and nutmeg wafted through the air. Shanice remembered that Renee loved baking sweet treats for her after a special evening of fun. "Do you really need flour," Shanice asked, "or do you want to keep her in suspense?"

Renee poured out two cups of coffee. "Whatever I want to do with Brandy is my business, not yours."

"Let's start again. Hi, Renee. How are you?"

"Fine, and yourself?"

"I'm doing all right." Unsure of how to ask about Lisa, Shanice decided to wade in slowly. "You're fine? I ran into one of your old friends and she said you were in trouble."

The singer tilted her head and part of her shoulder-length bob swept across her face. "You don't know any of my friends."

"I'd never met her before, but Barbara Robinson knew a lot about me."

Renee almost choked on the coffee. "Did she send you over here to harass me? She can go to hell."

Abandoning the idea to broach the subject gently, the story tumbled out of Shanice. "There are pictures floating around that suggest Ms. Barbara has an intimate relationship with your friend Lisa."

"Seriously?" Renee began chewing on her bottom lip.

Shanice took out the one picture the Robinsons had allowed her to have: a slightly out of focus Lisa leaning toward Ms. Barbara with a platter of steamed lobster and mussels between them. "See. I've looked at the whole bunch. No one is naked, but they get the point across."

"That is Lisa, but what does this have to do with me?"

"You and Ms. Barbara have a falling out, you introduce

her to Lisa, these pictures show up, and Lisa disappears. As far as Pastor Robinson and Ms. Barbara are concerned – all roads lead back to you."

"I don't have anything to do with this. You know me better than that."

"Do I?" Shanice shrugged. "Brandy and I could have acted out a bad scene in front of your neighbors."

Renee pushed her coffee cup away. "I wasn't thinking. I saw a chance to mess with you and make Brandy jealous."

"Ms. Barbara decided not to help advance your career; maybe this started as a nasty joke to mess with her?"

"I was upset, but I got a few auditions on my own. You are looking at the understudy for the lead of *A God Man Is Hard to Find*." Renee raised a hand over her head and struck a dramatic pose.

Shanice imagined an accident befalling the lead. "What about when you told her she was getting the nastiness she deserved?"

Renee sighed and slouched back in her seat. "Barbara called screaming about how she could ruin me. I hung up on her. You have to understand; I thought she was angry about the play." She closed her eyes. "If my success upset her, I wanted to rub her nose in it. Can't remember everything I said, but yeah – I left a message. Then I blocked her number."

Shanice cradled her cup. "I didn't really think you were involved," she confessed. "The Robinsons are promising to bring you down too, if those photos find their way to the media."

"You have to convince them that I have nothing to do with it."

"What can you tell me about Lisa?"

"Not much."

"I thought she was your friend."

"We hung out a few times, but she was never more than an acquaintance."

"You don't know anything about her at all?"

"I think she's a teacher – don't ask me where."

Shanice sighed. The trip was turning into a complete waste of time. "Speak to her recently?"

"No," Renee said. "After I introduced her to Barbara, Lisa cast me aside."

"I know what that's like." Shanice hoped a quick smile would take away the sting. It didn't.

"Do you?" Renee glared at her. "You didn't raise any objections when I told you the relationship was over."

"What choice did I have? When did we ever make joint decisions?"

"I told you the deal upfront about the restrictions on my love life. You knew exactly what to expect."

Concentrating on her lukewarm coffee, Shanice decided not to get baited into an argument. "I'll tell the Robinsons you aren't involved in this."

"If I wanted to threaten her, I wouldn't have to make anything up." A timer went off and Renee opened the oven door to inspect a tray of goodies. As she hovered over them, her full breasts threatened to spill out of the robe. "Want a cinnamon roll?"

Shanice stood up. "I don't need to be around when Brandy gets back."

"You don't think you could take her?"

"You're not worth the fight."

Shanice felt foolish and disposable. If she had been the one in trouble, would Renee have reached out to help her at all? The car sputtered and coughed beneath her, ready to take on Ardola's pothole challenge. Rather than go home, she set out toward the Chopin Cart. Shanice needed to talk to someone and she knew Debra would understand.

The gourmet grocery store was crowded and there was a line the delicatessen station. Though as manager she could have found an excuse to stay in the back office, Debra joined the fray behind the counter to help service customers. Her philosophy was let the subordinates see you get your apron dirty and they'll be less likely to kvetch when asked to do an unsavory task.

Shanice hovered in the dairy aisle until the customers thinned out. As she approached the deli, she saw Debra snap off her latex gloves. "Hey, big cheese," she called affectionately. "Do you have a minute?"

Debra hung up her apron and steered Shanice toward the store cafe. "I've been making platters for the last two hours. I need a break." She bought them both lattes. "What are you doing here?"

Shanice stretched before joining her friend on an extremely comfortable sofa. "I paid Renee a visit."

Debra rolled her eyes. "Don't tell me you had sex."

"No! I dropped by to thank her for the lead. She's the reason the Robinsons hired me." Then Shanice explained how she met Renee's new girlfriend.

"You're lucky that Brandy didn't pop you with a wrench." Laughing, Debra mock-punched Shanice in the jaw. "That's some soap opera mess."

"Caught me completely off-guard. Afterward, Renee acted nonchalant about the whole thing. Add that to the shady things she did when we were together… How did I get hooked up with a woman like that? What's wrong with me?"

"Sex or the possibility of it. That's the reason I get in trouble."

The barista listening to the conversation nodded in agreement. Shanice wondered how many confessions she had heard while filling the milk containers. "The messed up thing is that Renee broke up with me. If she hadn't let me go, I don't know how long I would have tried to stick it out with her."

"Don't worry about what might have been. Do you have to work with her for this web project?"

"No reason to see her again. It's done." Shanice crumpled her empty cup and tossed it in the trashcan. "Let's keep this between us, okay?"

"Sure." Tipping her head all the way back, Debra tapped out the last dregs of latte. "It's back to the trenches to me. Stay out of trouble, Sister Imogene."

Chapter 5

Shanice woke up with a renewed sense of purpose. She would find the Robinsons, relay the message from Renee, and spend the rest of her Sunday creating the website. Once she delivered the web templates, she could wash her hands of the affair. Then she could focus on growing her business and staying ahead of the rent. It was time to stop letting life happen to her.

Though the service did not start until 11:30, the parking lot of Hope Reborn Baptist Church was nearly full at 9 a.m. Rather than squeeze into a minuscule space, Shanice parked on a side street. The towering mass of stone and stained glass cast an impressive shadow over the deteriorating row houses around it. Except for the kids drawing a hopscotch grid on the sidewalk, the block was quiet.

This time around, Shanice decided against borrowing clothes. Her jeans and sneakers set her apart from the rest of the congregation. The usher who greeted her at the door looked confused when she strode in and began walking toward the sanctuary. "Sister, can I help you?"

"I'm looking for Pastor and Mrs. Robinson."

"The offices and common areas are downstairs."

Shanice descended the small staircase and saw an assortment of well-dressed children chasing each other around tables. The pastor's office was easy to find, but once inside, she encountered another gatekeeper. The nameplate on the desk introduced the new obstacle as Sarah Jeffries. Even though Sarah wore a very modest dress, her nails bespoke a much more exciting nightlife. They were a dark shade of purple with lavender flower petals arranged in a circle.

"Is Pastor Robinson in?" Shanice asked. "I need to see him."

"I'm sorry, Pastor Robinson is preparing for morning service." Sarah traced the edges of an appointment book with a sharp pencil. "Whatever the nature of your need, Deacon Michael can help you." Sarah couldn't have been more than thirty, but her sour/dour expression aged her considerably. The office was crowded but meticulous. Neat stacks of paper loomed in every corner. One ill-considered move could punish someone with a million paper cuts.

"My name is Shanice Wilkins. If you tell him I'm here, he'll want to see me."

"What's your business with our pastor?"

"That's his business, not yours."

As Sarah began rising out of her chair, Pastor Robinson opened the door to his inner sanctum. "Good morning, Ms. Wilkins." He extended a cold, clammy hand to her. He turned his smile to the secretary. "It's okay, Sarah."

"But, Pastor, Deacon Michael is here to help anyone who needs financial assistance."

Shanice sighed. She couldn't wait for this morning to be over.

Pastor Robinson sat on the edge of the desk. "You've got the wrong impression of Ms. Wilkins. She's our new web designer."

Sarah's eyes widened. "What?"

"It's time for Hope Reborn to extend and enhance its reach online. Beyond the public access channel, we need to get Sunday service to the masses."

Sarah couldn't hide her disappointment. "Internet outreach is my special project," she said. "I'm maintaining our social media pages. We can always post videos there."

"Social media networks are fine," Shanice said, "but there are more possibilities when you own your own space." Though she didn't care for the woman's attitude, she felt uncomfortable watching her squirm. "I'm only setting up the framework; the site will need to be maintained by the church."

"The Internet Ministry will still be your project," Pastor Robinson assured her. "We're just acquiring another tool. This way, Ms. Wilkins."

The women glared at each other one last time before Shanice followed him into the office. He closed the door behind her and put a finger to his lips. After a few seconds of silence, they heard a chair scrape against the floor. Pastor Robinson sighed. "She's going to sulk for a few minutes."

"Is she your secretary or security?" Shanice asked as she settled into a soft leather chair. She wished she had worn her loafers so she could slip off her shoes and burrow her toes in the deep pile carpeting. Her reflection beamed back from the polished cherrywood desk.

"A little of both," he said. "Sarah is here nearly every day keeping me on schedule, handling church business, and screening strangers who come in off the street. Every day, three or four people ask for money to buy groceries or keep the lights on."

"That sounds dangerous."

"It can be, so don't judge her too harshly." Pastor Robinson folded his hands. "Let's get to it. Have you talked to Renee?"

Shanice tried not to stare at his gray knuckles. He looked and smelled good but needed to moisturize. "I did, but shouldn't Ms. Barbara join us?"

"She's next door preparing for Sunday School. We'll walk over in a moment. I'm anxious to know where we stand."

"Renee has no idea what's going on. She hasn't seen Lisa in months."

He frowned. "What about the threatening message she left on voice mail?"

"That was a misunderstanding that had nothing to do with the blackmail scheme. Renee said if she wanted to hurt your Ms. Barbara, she wouldn't have to make something up." Shanice felt uncomfortable saying it.

"If it's not Renee, we definitely have a problem." He took off his glasses and rubbed his eyes. "A few weeks ago, someone left a profanity-filled letter for Barbara with our doorman."

"Did you go to the police?"

"No. We stopped going to the police years ago. It's one of the hazards of the job. Love letters come through the mail, notes accusing us of leading people to hell; anything that you can imagine. Usually, the vitriol is aimed at me. We put it out of our minds until the pictures showed up."

"If it's the same person, maybe there's a chance to catch them. Can you have the condo association check the security tapes?"

The minister shook his head. "Those cameras are attached to monitors that don't record a thing. All we know is that it was a woman who handed the doorman the envelope and he sees hundreds of people a day."

Shanice was out of ideas. "I'm sorry. There's nothing else I can do."

"This can't be a coincidence; Renee has to be involved somehow." He looked down at his watch. "Come on. We need to tell Barbara and develop a new course of action."

Shanice nearly had to run to keep up with the nimble man. He spoke to everyone as he walked by, but the hugs and kisses did not deter him. They didn't slow down until they were on the steps of the house next door. "This is part of the church?"

"Yes. Our building is big, but so is our congregation." The doorknob turned easily in his hand. Full of beanbag chairs, throw pillows, and sofas, the living room looked extremely comfortable. "Some of our smaller groups meet here and, after school, we have activities for local youth. Third floor is mostly storage. Children's Sunday school is on the second floor."

In the second-floor classroom, they found a desk and

chairs arranged in a haphazard circle waiting for students to arrive. There was no teacher. Pastor Robinson was confused. "She's obviously been here." He pointed at the blue bucket on the desk. "She washed the blackboard."

Shanice noticed pamphlets scattered across the floor. Her gaze followed them to a pool of crimson spreading from beneath the desk. "Look."

"Barbara!" The pastor ran to the front of the room and stopped cold. His mouth opened as if to gasp, but no sound came out.

Approaching from the other side, Shanice saw Barbara Robinson in a crumpled heap on the floor. Instinctively, she thought to take the woman's pulse but quickly drew back when she saw the deep gash in her head.

Pastor Robinson fell to his knees and pulled the body into his lap.

Shanice fumbled getting her phone and was momentarily stunned by a flash. A cavalcade of young voices forced her to regroup. She reached the door in time to keep three rowdy girls from entering. "There's no class today."

The children struggled to see around her. "What's wrong? What happened?"

Shanice pushed them away from the room. "Everything is okay, but we need an usher. Tell everyone class is canceled."

A little girl with braids grinned. "No class? It's the first time I got what I prayed for!"

Chapter 6

The usher alerted by the children, Elizabeth Johnson, had to see for herself what emergency warranted shutting down Sunday school. Then, with tears streaming down her face, she stood at the front door and prevented anyone else from entering until the police arrived. Back inside the church, she added her story to the rumors already circulating in the congregation.

Shanice hadn't been so lucky. After herding the children out and dealing with the skeptical usher, she waited on the creaking staircase. She felt guilty about leaving Pastor Robinson alone, but she couldn't go back in that room. The first pair of officers arrived quickly. They sequestered her in a first-floor classroom and went about securing the scene.

For what seemed like an eternity, she sat in an uncomfortable folding chair while an assortment of officers asked her variations of the same questions: Who are you? What happened? Why are you here? She stuck with the same story she told the secretary. It wasn't her place to say anything about the pictures or Renee. None of the officers called Barbara Robinson by her name. She had become "the victim" or, in some cases, "the body."

During breaks in questioning, Shanice tried desperately to focus her attention on anything that could push the memory of Ms. Barbara's twisted body out of her mind. Through heavy lace curtains, she took in the scene outside. The sidewalk in front of the annex had been cordoned off with yellow tape, keeping the devastated congregation at bay. A Channel 2 news van pulled up behind the coroner.

Instantly, a portion of the crowd gravitated to the television crew.

The only other visual distraction was an illustrated poster of a longhaired brown Jesus delighting little children and baby animals.

A familiar smell, cinnamon and sandalwood, wafted into the room. Shanice turned around to find a thick man with a thin mustache filling the doorway. Unlike the others, he wore a suit. "Ms. Wilkins? I'm Detective Gerard. I know you've already told your story, but I'd like you to go through it again with me." As he extended his hand, Shanice realized that he smelled like her father's aftershave lotion, but a razor hadn't been near Gerard's olive beige face that day. Sitting across the table from her, he took out a notepad and pen, and waited.

"Yesterday, Pastor and Mrs. Robinson hired me to revamp the church website. I dropped by his office today to clarify a few points about what they wanted. He thought Mrs. Robinson should be part of the conversation, so we came over here." Her eyes began burning, but there were no more tears to shed. "Then we found her."

Detective Gerard looked at her critically. "You look underdressed for Sunday service."

"I'm not a member of Hope Reborn."

"How did you know the Robinsons?"

"I didn't – not before yesterday."

"How did they come to hire you then?" He leered at her. "Are you sure you didn't know Pastor Robinson?"

Shanice ignored the insinuation. "I was recommended by a previous client."

"What was this burning question that couldn't wait until Monday?"

"The content management software I recommended to them requires a MySQL database and I wanted them to understand that they would need to upgrade the package they have with their current hosting company. I wanted them to understand that it would be a different and separate cost."

The detective's eyes started to glaze over and he lifted his hands in surrender. "Okay, Ms. Wilkins, no need to get into it. Fine. You couldn't handle that with a call?"

"I also wanted to pick up a DVD of a recent service so I could cull audio and video files."

"Did they know you were coming?"

"No. This was supposed to be a quick stop over before brunch." As if on cue, her phone began vibrating in her pocket. It had been going off every few minutes, but she didn't dare answer it. She wouldn't be able to tell the whole story with the police around – which would have made her roommates more anxious than they needed to be. Hopefully, they would take the hint and start eating without her.

"How did the pastor react to you showing up?"

"Surprised but not upset or anything. His secretary gave me the third degree. She got upset; we waited for her to leave. We talked about her for moment." As soon as the words flew from her lips, Shanice wished she could take them back. She was talking too much.

"What did he say about her?"

"Nothing really."

"Let me be the judge of that."

As much as she didn't like Sarah, Shanice didn't want to throw suspicion on her or anyone. "She thought I came off the street looking for a handout. It pissed me off. It amused Pastor Robinson, though. Anyway, when I started to ask about the website, he stopped me because he wanted Ms. Barbara to hear it too. Then we came over here. "

"Was there anyone else outside?"

"There were a few people down the block, but no one running or doing anything unusual."

"Did he have to unlock the door?"

Shanice thought back. "No. He had to really give the door a shove to open it, but he didn't have to use a key. We went straight to the second floor classroom."

"What happened after you got there?"

Shanice sighed. "The room looked empty at first. If we had walked by, we wouldn't have known anyone was in there. Her purse and Bible were on the desk and pamphlets – Sunday school tracts – were all over the floor. That's when I saw the blood. We went around the desk and..." Involuntarily, Shanice's left hand went up to her mouth. "She was almost under it. Pastor Robinson ran to her and I stood there."

Shanice had started crying without realizing it. Detective Gerard looked away while she fumbled through her pockets for a tissue. "I'm sorry. I've never seen anything like that before." She paused. "Then I stopped the children from coming in and called 911."

"And the usher?"

"I sent for her because I wanted her to keep other kids out of the building."

"And what did you do?"

"I sat on the steps until the police arrived."

"Anyone else inside the house?"

A chill went through Shanice. "I don't know."

He closed his notebook. "Thank you, Ms. Wilkins. That will be all for the moment." He handed her a business card. "If you remember anything else, please let me know. Any questions?"

"Who could do something like this?"

"It happens all the time, Ms. Wilkins. People can be triggered by anything: anger, love, money."

Shanice took another look at the throng outside the front door. "Is there another way out of here?"

"You don't want your fifteen minutes?" He seemed genuinely amused. "Sure, you can go out the back door." He walked her to the kitchen and gave a nod to the policeman stationed near the stove.

After a couple of wobbly steps and a quick sprint across an overgrown walkway, she stood in the church parking lot. Though alone, she couldn't shake the feeling that someone was staring at her.

A thoughtful parishioner had wedged a stick under the side door to keep it from closing. People gathered in the hall cried and consoled each other. Consumed with grief, no one paid attention as Shanice walked across the room and slipped into the pastor's office.

Sarah sobbed quietly at her desk. Next to her stood an older woman who alternated between rubbing and patting her shoulder. The pens and paper clips were in disarray. The secretary dried her tear-streaked face. "Is her body battered up like people have been saying?" she asked.

The elder's voice was stronger than her minuscule frame. "She was cut up something terrible. Stabbed ten or eleven times." She wore a wide-brimmed feathered hat that looked on the verge of swallowing her up whole.

Sarah pointed at Shanice. "She was there, Mother Banks. She and Pastor Robinson found the body."

The door swung open and an ashen-faced woman rushed in. Drawing a large coat tight around her trembling shoulders, she looked like she would shake apart. "Is it true? Is Ms. Barbara dead?"

Mother Banks checked that Sarah was all right before throwing her arms around the newcomer. "It's true, Cheryl. Some maniac attacked her while she was getting ready for Sunday school."

Cheryl pulled away, her face twisted in terror. "Were any of the children hurt?"

"No," Mother Banks assured her. "Barbara was the only one there."

As Cheryl exhaled, the tears began flowing. "I went to Sister Claritha's house to offer her communion when she got the call about Ms. Barbara."

Drying her eyes, Sarah flipped through a calendar on the desk. "That's not right," she said. "Deaconess Ophelia was supposed to take communion to the sick and shut-ins this week. Is she here?" The church administrator was back.

Embarrassed, Cheryl looked away. "Ophelia met me in the parking lot and asked me to do her this favor. I think she had a rough night--"

Mother Banks shushed her and motioned toward Shanice. This conversation could wait. "Cheryl, this is the young lady who called for help. She was about to tell us what she saw next door."

With everyone staring at her, Shanice once again felt eyes of judgment sweeping over her not-quite-ready-for-church ensemble. She took a perverse pleasure in discovering that, beneath the coat, Cheryl's pale blue dress was frayed at the neck. Not ready for another interrogation, she lied. "I barely saw anything."

"Who are you?" Cheryl demanded.

"Wait," said Sarah. "She went into the pastor's inner sanctum and emerged with three paper cups filled with water. "Deaconess Cheryl, Mother Banks, this is Shanice Wilkins. She is helping us out with the Internet ministry."

Shanice extended her hand and received two limp handshakes in return. The deaconess wasn't through evaluating her yet. She adjusted her coat and looked down her nose. "Where did Pastor Robinson find you?"

"Let the young woman be," Mother Banks said. "I'm sure she's been through a lot this morning."

Shanice was thankful for the reprieve. "Can I leave a note for Pastor Robinson?"

"Of course." Sarah gave her a pen and a notepad.

Knowing it would be scrutinized, Shanice was careful with her message. *Pastor Robinson, there are no words to express my deep sorrow for your loss. We can definitely put any plans for the site on hold.* She folded the note and handed it to Sarah.

"We're not safe," Deaconess Cheryl was saying as Shanice closed the door behind her. "I know the church is supposed to be a community resource, but we need to have a balance between doing outreach and protecting ourselves."

Shanice ducked out of the side door and walked around the corner to join the crowd that had assembled outside of the church. Sequestered in the annex, she wanted nothing more than to escape back home to the safety of her own bed. Now she was curious.

Working her way through the crowd, she heard wailing, screams, and prayers.

To get a better view, she decided to cross the street and mingle with the residents who had come out on their stoops. Although it appeared a chaotic mass at first, the church folk split into four groups. The majority had gathered at the perimeter of the crime tape, clutching tissues and tittering anxiously every time the annex door opened. Directly in front of the church, an older gentleman in a tight black suit led a group in prayer. Eyes closed and pompadour shaking, his voice carried. "The Devil is busy, Lord, but we know that you are the source of our strength."

Others focused their attention on roving reporter Janine Sampson. After a few sips from a Styrofoam cup, she exchanged her drink for a microphone and waited for her cue. The always-peppy personality looked older in person.

New people arrived, looking shell-shocked, and were drawn into one of these enclaves. With every new disclosure of the tragedy, there was a new cry of terror.

The people Shanice stood with were not quiet observers. In snatches of conversation, she heard a variety of rumors and theories being born.

"Bet it was a pervert hiding in one of the rooms, ready to snatch up a little girl."

"Probably caught one of those deacons doing dirty. I don't like it when old men get too familiar."

"Don't know why they leave that door open."

"Bet it was that fool who tried to snatch Tonya's purse last week."

An elderly man stepped gingerly as he approached the curb. "What's happening here?"

The news would have literally knocked him back if a

young woman hadn't been there to help steady him. "Oh no, not Ms. Barbara. She's a real sweetheart – always smiling and inviting people in. I used to tell her I had a little more sinnin' to do." He chuckled at the memory and then blinked back tears. "God let something like that happen to her, then we all in trouble."

Chapter 7

The door jerked open before Shanice put her key in the lock. A tearful Gina pulled her inside. "What happened?"

Still in her pajamas, Debra cradled a bowl of cereal. She pointed her spoon at the television. "It's coming on again."

Janine Sampson wore a solemn expression. "This morning, tragedy struck the congregation of Hope Reborn Baptist Church. The body of Barbara Robinson, wife of Pastor Walter Robinson, was found in an empty classroom moments before students were due to arrive for Sunday school. There is confusion and outrage in Griffin Hill that such a beloved leader could fall victim to such a vicious attack."

The segment jumped to a pre-recorded interview with the leader of the prayer group, now identified as Maynard Perkins. "You know, Ms. Barbara would want us to reach out to him, a soul crying out for help." Shaking his head, he patted his moist cheeks with a handkerchief. "It's a challenge not to be consumed with anger and – quite frankly – with hatred for whoever did this. It's a pain that cuts deep. She would have done anything to help a person in need. It's just senseless violence."

Gina rubbed her eyes with a balled-up tissue. "I can't believe this. How could someone hurt Ms. Barbara? She went out of her way to help everyone. There are truly evil people in this world."

The camera panned the crowds and Shanice slipped in and out of frame.

Deb turned down the volume. "That's you! What were

you doing in the middle of everything?"

Shanice dropped down on the sofa and put her head in her hands. "I was with the pastor when he found her."

"What? Are you okay?" Gina asked, sitting down next to her.

"Yeah, I think so. I've never seen anyone hurt before and I don't want to see it again." Shanice sighed heavily and leaned into her landlord's embrace.

"Everybody says it's horrific," Debra said, "but no one is giving any details. Was she stabbed, shot or what? Why were you even down there?"

Gina shot her a nasty look. "Debra! Give Shanice time to catch her breath. I'm sure she'll talk about it when she's ready."

Shanice wiped the back of her hand across her tearing eyes. "I told you, Pastor Robinson hired me to revamp their website."

Debra knew she should stop, but Gina fawning over Shanice was too much. "You wouldn't approach a client dressed like that. And no one is buying that you wanted to thank Renee so much that you needed to tell her in person. What's the deal?" She hadn't meant to let the secret slip, but she didn't regret it.

Gina pulled away. "What's going on? Are you in some kind of trouble? You usually don't lie." Though never spoken, the words "to me" hung in the air like a thick fog between them.

Looking down at her nervous hands, Shanice struggled with how much to reveal. "If I tell you something, you have to swear not to tell anyone else." Her roommates looked at each other and nodded. Shanice continued. "The website was only part of the reason they hired me. Ms. Barbara was convinced that Renee had played a nasty prank on her. They wanted me to deliver a message to her and I did."

"Why did they go to you?" Gina asked. "I don't understand."

"They were close friends of Renee at one time. They

knew all about me – even how I handled Stonetalker1769. Ms. Barbara thought if anyone could reason with her, it would be me."

"Stone who?" asked Gina.

Debra set her bowl down. "Let me tell it. Renee's sister, Renita, met a guy online named StoneTalker1769. They started talking on the phone and, a few weeks later, she fell in love. He started whining about money problems and Renita whipped out the checkbook. When Renee couldn't talk any sense into her, she asked Shanice to check him out."

"StoneTalker1769 thought he was slick," Shanice said. "He called from a private number. Smart, right? But he used the same user name in gaming forums and product reviews. After a few searches, I found his real name. The address was easy after that."

Debra started laughing. "Orlando Buris of Cumberland Pointe. That's when Shanice and I took a little road trip."

Gina folded her arms. "Please don't tell me you two went there to start mess."

"We were looking for evidence he was a conman. All we did was take pictures." Debra crossed her heart with the spoon. "Dude claimed he shared a small studio with his disabled mother. He had a regular townhouse and a wife."

"Did the sister feel like a fool?" Gina asked.

"Of course not," Debbie responded. "Women like that never do. She made excuses for him and cussed us out."

Shanice closed her eyes. She had taken pictures of StoneTalker1769. What had Ms. Barbara said? *Someone else held the camera.* Had the Robinsons thought she was Renee's accomplice? Were they warning her at the same time they wanted her to warn Renee? The exorbitant fee the pastor offered – was it a payoff?

"What did Renee do to them?" asked Gina. "Start a scandal in the choir?"

"The Robinsons received a package of photos showing Ms. Barbara having dinner with a young woman, a friend of Renee. There were pictures taken in her hotel suite. The shots suggested intimacy. Ms. Barbara assumed Renee was behind it because they'd had a falling out."

Debra pitched forward. "Pictures of them in bed together?"

Gina's eyes widened. "Are you saying that Barbara Robinson, the first lady of Hope Reborn Baptist Church, was having an affair with a woman?" She started laughing. "That's ridiculous."

"No!" Shanice felt her chest tighten. "No one was in the hotel room. It was pictures of Ms. Barbara's nightgown on the bed. She didn't sleep with anyone. The Robinsons wanted me to kill a rumor before it got started. This is exactly why I didn't want to tell you."

"Calm down," Debra said. "It doesn't go any further than this room. Finish the story." She smirked. "Tell Gina about the warm welcome you received at Renee's place. Open robe and cinnamon rolls."

Gina put up a hand, her eyes radiating disappointment. "I don't need to know everything. Cut to the chase. Is that why you went back to the church today?"

"Yeah." Shanice avoided her gaze. "I came by to let them know that Renee isn't involved."

"Tell the police?" Gina asked.

"Of course not. I told them what I initially told you. That has nothing to do with Ms. Barbara's murder."

"Smart move," Debra said. "Something like that gets into a police report, it will definitely be leaked – wife of prominent minister in lesbian scare."

Shanice's phone began ringing and Renee's face appeared on the screen. Gina stood up and stretched. "Looks like your girl heard the news."

"It's not like that. I swear." Shanice silenced the phone and accidentally opened the camera app. The last pictures were taken at awkward angles, featuring blurry fingers in front of the classroom of horror. She had accidentally taken pictures of the scene. "Oh my God."

Debra grabbed the phone and swiped through the

images. "Whoa!" The blood on the desk drove home the gruesome reality of violence. "Need some air. I'll be right back." Dropping the phone on the table, she went out on the front porch and fought to keep her breakfast down.

Gina took the phone and put it face down on the table. "The police don't know you have these, do they? You should tell them. "

"No." Shanice put her head in her hands. "Delete them, please. It's already seared in my brain; I don't want that energy around me."

"The drama you can keep to yourself, but this could be evidence. Didn't you talk to a police detective? Let him tell you it's not important."

"I'm not talking to Gerard again. He suggested I was sleeping with Pastor Walter. That man is old enough to be my grandfather."

Gina chuckled. "I told you about the rumors. You'd be surprised how many women find him attractive. It's about power, not looks. Ms. Barbara didn't tolerate that kind of foolishness."

The phone rang again; Renee reappeared on the screen. Gina began gathering the soiled tissue. "You'll figure out everything," she said. "Just be careful. Better take that call before Renee runs down your battery." She picked up Debra's dirty cereal bowl and left.

Shanice sighed and turned off the phone. The truth was bringing nothing but grief. She found Gina in the kitchen, lining up celery on a cutting board. "Listen, I didn't go over there expecting anything from Renee. I thought she should know what the Robinsons were accusing her of."

"It's all right," Gina said without turning around. "It's not really my business what you do or want from Renee."

Folding her arms, Shanice leaned against the deep freezer. "As much complaining as I did when we were together, you'd be right to suck your teeth if I was trying to get with Renee again. Even if she served herself to me on a gold platter, I wouldn't want her."

"You're lying." Gina hit her with an oven mitt and laughed.

"Nope. I'm moving forward, not backward. I thought an old friend was in trouble and wanted to help." The tension gone, Shanice's dimples were in full force. "Am I still your favorite tenant?"

"It's Debra's turn this week." Gina reached for a knife and began dicing. "Does Pastor Robinson know your camera went off?"

"Maybe. The flash went off once, but I'm sure he wasn't focused on me."

"Still, if he remembers and tells the police, it will look bad that you didn't say anything."

Shanice scoffed. "I'm not calling Detective Gerard."

Gina smiled mischievously. "He's not the only policeman in the world."

Chapter 8

When Gina met Juanita Childress at the home of a mutual friend, the chemistry between them was undeniable. Gina invited her out several times, but there were always scheduling conflicts. The police academy student didn't have time. The nervous energy brought forth by their attraction had tamped down over the years, but it hadn't entirely disappeared. They had a comfortable friendship now.

The fondness Offer Childress felt for Gina did not extend to Shanice and Debra. Leaning against the sink, she clicked through the grainy images and cast a weary glance at Shanice. "Taking pictures; that's your first impulse upon seeing a body?"

"Of course not. That side button is programed to activate the camera app." Peppermint tea smoothed the edges of Shanice's quivering stomach. "It tends to go off when I take my phone out of my pocket."

"Explains why there are so many pictures of your palm. This thing is ancient. Can you get the images off of here? Don't edit them in any way, not even to make them clearer." Childress handed the phone back to Shanice.

"No problem." Shanice finished her tea and went up to her room.

Gina put another kettle of water on the stove. "You really think those pictures are valuable?"

Childress shrugged. "Not my call. Gerard will definitely want to take a close look at clues volunteered by the prime suspect."

"That's not funny. That detective went out of his way to make her feel uncomfortable."

"It's an interview technique. Put a little pressure on the witness, gauge the behavior, and figure out if you're talking to a potential suspect. Gerard probably treated Pastor Robinson with kid gloves today, but I'm sure he's going to get some hard questions too."

"It's not fair to antagonize people who are already dealing with trauma. Shanice didn't know who the Robinsons were until Friday."

"She probably doesn't have anything to worry about. I, on the other hand, am worried that we'll be collecting Social Security before I finish renovating the basement. I thought you were calling to fire me."

"It's coming along. You cleaned out the back and fixed the pantry shelves." *And you are free,* Gina thought. She was saving thousands letting the policewoman, a former carpenter, take on the project on her days off. "Good work is better than fast work."

Shanice came back and held out a memory card. "Here you go."

"Sorry I teased you earlier." Childress softened her voice. "I know you had a rough time this morning, but don't take it personally. How did you get hooked up in this mess anyway?"

"Website and social media consultation," Shanice said. "If we had gotten there a few minutes earlier, this might not have happened."

Childress touched her shoulder. "Or Gerard could have had three bodies to deal with instead of one. You can't rewrite the past, so don't try."

Alone in her room, Shanice thought the tears would come. When they didn't, she turned on the television and tried to concentrate on a *Jeffersons* marathon. Renee had sounded wounded in the voice mail messages, crying as if Barbara Robinson was her closest friend in the world. That return call could wait until tomorrow.

Debra stopped by to mumble an apology. Gina checked in on her occasionally and tried to entice her to eat. Despite their concern and offers of comfort, Shanice felt alone. She didn't know what to say.

Shanice played with the idea of calling her parents, but her mother always knew when something was wrong. Mama would strongly suggest that she come home. Within minutes, Shanice would be desperately looking for an excuse to hang up.

After a few hours, she gave in to the temptation to boot up her laptop and check the local news. An unnamed police source revealed that a person of interest was being questioned. Even better, her name did not appear in any of the articles. Her involvement had been summed up in a brief sentence: Pastor Walter Robinson was with a parishioner when they found his wife's body in a classroom.

Knowing that Detective Gerard had a real suspect to badger was a relief. She went to bed believing that justice would be done.

Sleep did come, but not peace. In her dreams, Shanice walked up a creaky staircase to a hallway full of doors. It was easy to recognize the door to the Sunday school room – a small pool of slow, sticky blood seeped under it. Whether she went back down the steps or chose another door, she always came face to face with that door. Then she decided to stand still. The pooling blood gathered itself into a stream, threatening to engulf everything in its path.

Chapter 9

The next morning, Shanice found herself in the kitchen doing a scavenger hunt for breakfast. The refrigerator offered two-day-old pork fried rice, but her stomach grumbled in disapproval. Not in the mood to cook, she poured chocolate syrup into a container of peanut butter and spread the mixture on Ritz crackers, completed the makeshift meal with a glass of milk, and planted herself on the sofa.

Footsteps scrambling overhead meant that Gina was up and, as usual for Monday morning, running late. Clad in a muted gray skirt set, she appeared at the bottom of the staircase clutching a pair of purple heels. "Have you seen my purse?" she asked while straightening her stockings.

Shanice pointed at the recliner and the over-sized, all-purpose canvas bag Gina used for work. "Good morning to you too," she said.

Gina stuck out her tongue and then smiled. "How are you feeling?"

"I'm good. The police have a real suspect, so I've moved on. My focus is on making the Hope Reborn website." That wasn't completely true. In between nightmares, Shanice worried police would check the Robinson's financial records. How would she justify taking money from them up front when her website clearly offered a free consultation?

"Y'all went to Sapphic Sunday, right?" Shanice asked. "How was it?"

Gina fished a makeup case out of her purse and applied purple gloss to her lips. "I enjoyed myself. Debra held up the wall and rolled her eyes when I accepted invitations to dance. I tried to get her out on the floor a couple of times, but that was futile."

After confirming cosmetic perfection, Gina slid a couple of silver bracelets on each arm. "Be gentle with yourself today. I won't say anything if one of my bath bombs goes missing." She kissed Shanice on the forehead before disappearing into the morning sun.

Unlike Gina, Debra was fully dressed for work – khaki pants and a fitted white shirt bearing the Chopin Cart emblem – when she made her appearance. "Don't get crumbs in my spot."

Shanice shoved another cracker in her mouth.

Debra's laughter trailed behind her as she went into the kitchen. She returned with orange juice and a plate of cold pork fried rice. "Good to see you back to your old self."

"This weekend was a weird diversion, but it's back to the grind for me."

After downing her juice, Debra lapsed into her normal multi-tasking AM routine. Her left hand wielded the fork, while her right alternated between scrolling through text messages and television channels. Both hands stilled as she blushed.

The pause only lasted a moment, but Shanice couldn't let it go by unnoticed. "Somebody from last night?"

"Nah, I didn't get any play last night. Gina mean-mugged anybody who looked in my direction." Debra ran a hand over her head, noting the newly grown stubble. "The ladies I approached were put off by her hovering around."

"Yeah, I'm sure that's the way it went down." Shanice decided to let it go. "Who was that?"

"A friend showing off her new bathing suit. Anyway, let's get back to you. We need to think of a way to use this incident to get publicity for your business. Talk to a reporter about finding the body; you'll get a lot of new eyes to your website. Bet you pick up some new customers."

Shanice frowned. "A few people would be curious

enough to want a free consultation, but it wouldn't lead to actual work."

"Get rid of the free consultation for the time being. Make people pay for the privilege of your time." Debra used her tongue to dislodge a piece of rice that had stationed itself in the right corner of her mouth. "Don't worry; you keep pushing forward with the business and the kinks will work themselves out."

"Thanks. I'll think about it." Shanice had considered adding churches to her list of target customers, but she had no intention of luring them in with Barbara Robinson's death.

Debra threw her apron over her shoulder. "I'm off to cut the cheese." The dishes she left on the table rattled when she slammed the door.

Shanice felt her relationship with Debra shifting and she didn't like it. Since she moved in, there were snide remarks, but only when Gina was around. Yesterday, at her most vulnerable, Debra betrayed her trust.

It made no sense. Though Gina flirted lightly with them, she was clear about not dating tenants. Tiptoeing around Debra's feelings wasn't working. The trio could be having fun when anything – a smile or a laugh – could prompt Debra to stomp away. They needed to confront her, sit down, and talk it out.

After clearing away breakfast crumbs, Shanice set up her laptop on the dining room table. She started with a generic HTML template. For sample content, she pieced together material from the myriad Hope Reborn social media pages. Ms. Barbara's presence in the church was undeniable. Losing the fight to stay focused, Shanice's thoughts drifted back to her appeal for help.

Who was Lisa Whitmore and why did she target Barbara? A Google search resulted in thousands of hits. Narrowing the search by city and age didn't help. Had she worked alone or did someone else direct her to infiltrate the

Robinsons' inner circle? Whatever the reason, the scheme had to be over now. With Ms. Barbara dead, there was no one to blackmail. All that effort for nothing.

Her phone rang and she was happy for the distraction. A weak, raspy voice greeted her. "Ms. Wilkins, it's Walter Robinson."

Shanice was speechless, then finally managed to say, "I'm so sorry. Are you okay?"

"I've presided over hundreds of funerals; part of my mission is to console people. I thought I understood grief. To have someone taken away from you; this is a different kind of weight." His voice thinned out to a whisper. "It's almost unbearable."

"Is there anything I can do?"

"Yes. Continue searching for Lisa. You can't slander the dead. This woman can say or do anything without fear of retribution. Find her. Find the person who took those pictures."

Shanice needed to know. "You thought it was me. Renee told you about how I took pictures of her sister's lover, so you thought I took the pictures of Ms. Barbara."

"Renee loved to talk about her network, so we thought it was possible," he conceded. "If you were involved, we had hoped to scare you into ending the foolishness. If you weren't involved, you could let her know how high the stakes were. After you left, both of us agreed that you were unlikely to be involved."

Pastor Robinson was suddenly interrupted; the sound of murmurs punctuated with sobs filled the background. He consoled his visitors. After a few moments, it sounded like he was alone again. "They don't really understand," he said. "Barbara didn't sit on the sidelines to offer me aid and comfort. We were in the trenches together." He took a deep breath and composed himself. "Ms. Wilkins, I want to protect her legacy."

"There's really nothing else I can do."

"Renee stopped by earlier and promised to help. She said

if you stopped by her studio, she can point you in the right direction."

Shanice didn't want to do it, but a little more information – maybe even a zip code – could whittle down the search results and find the real Lisa Whitmore. Plus, didn't her newly replenished checking account demand that she do more?

"Okay. I'll try talking to Renee again."

Chapter 10

Shanice had dried off from a shower and was hunting through the laundry basket to find a pair of matching socks when the thought suddenly hit her: *Renee has a studio?*

She went to Renee's website. While the template Shanice had set up remained the same, new pages had been added and the footnote link to Wilkins Web Design and Consulting had disappeared. Whoever altered the site had tinkered with the code – which meant that Renee had played the naive technophobe with someone else. A flash of jealousy caught Shanice by surprise.

The new Lift Your Voice section contained full details about Renee's new endeavor. Why settle for making a joyful noise when you can receive voice lessons from the diva herself? There were a variety of affordable "praise packages" for everyone from choral members to aspiring soloist. Lessons occurred in a professional rehearsal space in an area that had ample parking. Renee promised her technique could push past emotional blocks and unleash a voice that would ring out strong and harmoniously for the Lord.

To underscore her authority as a teacher, there was a slideshow of Renee visiting various music venues. Shanice had taken those pictures herself – not too long before they broke up. With a borrowed camera, they took snaps in the vestibule of the Peabody Institute, in front of Scalang Hall and at a piano in the School of Rhythm and Blues. Renee did not claim affiliation with any of the institutions; she said it wasn't her fault if people made assumptions.

They had used The Grey Pamplemousse, a local

hangout known for its eclectic customers, as a home base. The tiny eatery known for its eccentric window display – a ceramic grapefruit on a pedestal being worshiped by an assortment of broken Barbie dolls – bustled at night, when tipsy club kids and the tourists who gawked at them competed for table space.

At one in the afternoon, it was nearly empty. Renee used the restroom for her various wardrobe changes. For the first time, they were out in public together without the burden of fear or anxiety.

Foolishly, Shanice had suggested they round the day out by going to the movies. With those few reckless words, their happy afternoon was over. The immediate response was a disappointed sigh followed by chilly silence. Trying to back pedal only deepened the frown lines spreading across Renee's brow. "You had to ruin this, didn't you?" Even now, the words were like a cold slap in the face.

Shanice wrote down the address of the studio. This time around, she would talk to Gina before seeing her ex to stave off any future misunderstanding.

A seven-story building of mirrored glass and steel housed The Waybert-Slone Foundation. In the main lobby, iron sculptures twisted into humanoid shapes surrounded a heart-shaped fountain.

Though Lydia the receptionist juggled two phone lines, she waved Shanice through. "Gina has a workshop, but if you hurry, you can catch her before it starts." Lydia used her elbow to gesture down a corridor. "Room 5B."

Shanice sprinted down the hall and slipped into the back of a packed conference room. Stretched out before her was a sea of toupees, bald spots, and thinning comb-overs. Some heads sported all three.

Gina was at the helm, chatting with people in the first row and distributing handouts. The cut of her gray suit flattered her curves without being suggestive. When speaking before a crowd, Gina believed wardrobe was paramount to getting and keeping the audience's attention.

Shanice caught her eye just as the lights dimmed. A slide came into focus on the wall behind the presenters: "Helping LGBTQ Clients Find the Gold at the End of the Rainbow."

"Good afternoon, everyone." Gina took her place behind the podium and greeted the audience with a big, bright smile. "LGBTQ people can face unique challenges when it comes to financial planning and it's encouraging to see so many professionals interested in serving our community better. First, I'd like to tell you a little about Waybert-Slone. The best way to explain what our organization does is to explain how it helped me."

The title dissolved into a sepia-toned photograph of a young couple – one woman in a man's suit with her face partially obscured by a fedora and the other in a dress that showed no skin but left little to the imagination. Gina took a sip of water before launching into her personal story. "My Great Aunt Mavis and her partner Ellie had been together over fifty years. They met when they were in their early twenties and were inseparable. Working in the same clothing factory, they had to keep their relationship a secret. They kept separate apartments and went on public dates with a male couple that they knew."

In the next photo, they were older and posing in front of their house. They wore knee-length winter coats. Ellie was adjusting her hat while Mavis brushed snow from her afro. "Fast forward to the late seventies. They moved into a house in Maynard Wood. By now, Aunt Mavis and Ellie had stopped making excuses for being single. It didn't take long before neighbors realized that they were what my mother calls 'special friends.' Not everyone wanted them there, but most people were indifferent.

"Not long after their sixtieth anniversary, we found out Ellie had stomach cancer. Both of their families were supportive. We ran errands, helped clean the house, etc. We did what families do. After the funeral, Ellie's sister let Aunt Mavis know that she had their deepest sympathies and assured her that they didn't expect her to move right away.

The house had been in Ellie's name, so she assumed she would inherit what little estate there was."

There were a couple of murmurs and Gina waited a beat to let it sink in. "Aunt Mavis wasn't on the deed, but the will left everything to her. Ellie's sister had a lawyer and was prepared to fight. My great aunt was terrified. She had just lost the love of her life and, at the whim of a judge, could lose her home. She reached out to me, a newly out lesbian who everyone else in the family was whispering about. I turned to Waybert-Slone. They put us in touch with a lawyer who had experience defending similar suits and was willing to waive his usual fees. A true family service organization, Waybert-Slone encouraged Aunt Mavis to join a gay and lesbian seniors group. Ultimately, the case was decided in her favor.

"Watching my great aunt struggling to navigate the legal system is what inspired me to pursue a career in public service. In particular, I wanted to help the organization that helped us. Our goal here at Waybert-Slone is to make sure that all families – even the non-traditional ones – get full, equal treatment under the law. I never want to hear a story about blood relatives using their biological link to destroy chosen families.

"I know what you're thinking. 'People can get married, Gina. It's a different world.' Not like it was in Aunt Mavis' day.' There are many issues left to tackle. For example, what's the benefit of marriage in a state where you can be fired for your sexual orientation? We here at Waybert-Slone believe in recognizing and celebrating milestones, but it's not time to drop the baton. There is a pot of gold, but we haven't reached it yet.

"That's my story. Now I would like to introduce you to Meredith White. She's the woman who picked up the phone when this confused nineteen-year-old was looking for help. Now she's our executive director. "

As Meredith took center stage, Gina slipped up the side aisle and Shanice fell in behind her. Once in the hallway,

Gina turned on her heels. "What's happening?"

"I wanted to ask your advice about something."

"You could have called."

"Yeah, but then I wouldn't get a chance to see you."

Gina looked at her watch. "I'm back on in a moment. We can flirt or you can get down to business."

"Pastor Robinson wants me to continue looking for Lisa. There's another lead he wants me to run down and I feel obligated to see this through."

"That's understandable. Do what you must but be careful. If it gets dangerous or too weird, promise me you'll call Childress."

"I'm glad you understand." Shanice braced herself for a rebuke. "That's only part of it, though."

"I've got to go. Tell Renee I said, 'Hi.'"

"How did you know I was going to see her?"

"I didn't." With that, Gina winked and disappeared back into the conference room.

Chapter 11

Renee's studio was in the Gretchen building, a mixture of rehearsal and office space anchored by a gourmet coffee shop that doubled as an avant-garde gallery. Shanice bit tentatively into a fudge cookie with choco-jalapeno chips while an artist's erotic reinterpretation of the *Mona Lisa* glared angrily from above. Neither seduced her appetite, so she continued on.

Though the ornate nameplate on the door was impressive, Renee's space was claustrophobic. Shanice walked into the room and almost collided with a fake plant. The nicest thing in the reception area was an executive leather chair, stationed behind a plain desk. Brochures detailing Renee's services were spread out like a fan atop the desk; in the middle was a candy dish full of lemon-ginger lozenges.

The rear wall had a half-length window that revealed the actual rehearsal studio. Renee was giving a young client a verbal workout, so Shanice grabbed a piece of candy and tried to get comfortable on a metal folding chair. Despite the soundproof room, it was obvious that the instructor was having a devil of a time pulling the performance she wanted from the frustrated student. Both were relieved when the session was over.

As she walked into the reception area, the girl pulled a pink backpack over her pencil-thin shoulders and tossed a piece of gum into her mouth. She barely glanced at Shanice before looking back at her teacher. "Ms. Renee, can we work on a modern song next time? I'm tired of 'The Old Rugged

Cross.' What does 'rugged' mean anyway?"

Renee hid her anger behind a tight smile. "Maleka, you need to ground yourself in the foundations of gospel. There will be plenty of time for pop songs once you nail down the classics."

Sighing heavily, Maleka put her earphones on and went out to ignore the world.

Shanice laughed. "It's okay if she's off key. The Lord knows her heart."

Renee dropped into her chair and retrieved a small oscillating fan from under the desk. "Her mother wants her to outshine everyone else in choir, but I can only do so much."

"How long have you had this space?"

"A few months. Giving private lessons in people's homes was fine when it was just the women I met through my workshops. Strangers started contacting me and it felt a little creepy. Brandy made a few calls and here I am at a very reasonable rate. Speaking of calls, why haven't you been returning mine? Why did you show up unannounced?"

"After the police and my roommates, I didn't feel like rehashing the story again." Shanice savored the last of the cough drop. "Besides, I didn't want to give you the chance to set up another welcoming committee."

Leaning into the breeze, Renee closed her eyes. "I didn't plan for you and Brandy to meet. She was on her way out but changed her mind when she realized I was expecting company. That's when I lied and told her it was church business; anything to get rid of her. She insisted on hanging around and got her feelings hurt." She shrugged. "You know how I feel about lovers overstepping boundaries, but I decided to let her have her way."

"Right. Why were you still wearing a robe? You knew what Brandy would think. One of us could have been hurt."

"Please, Brandy isn't a threat. It was a lesson she needed to learn. She's the kind of woman who does you a favor and then assumes her sphere of influence goes beyond the bedroom. My business is still my business. I think she got the message."

"I wish you had found some other way to communicate that to her."

Renee sucked her teeth. "I'm sorry, okay? Let it go. I know you've been through a lot lately but antagonizing me won't make it better." She began rearranging her brochures. "Now, is it true what the news is saying? It was a vagrant or some deranged drug addict?"

"The police haven't told me anything."

"Did you say anything to them about that disagreement I had with Barbara?"

Shanice shook her head. "No." *I got involved in this mess to save you, not turn you in.* "Do you really have info about Lisa or were you trying to score points with Pastor Robinson?"

"I wasn't completely truthful before. I was Lisa's vocal coach. She wants to sing, but at the same time, she doesn't want to draw attention to herself. She paid for eight lessons up front. I still have her application." Stretching, Renee rifled through the drawer of a filing cabinet. "It's not much, but there could be something in it that can help. You're good at finding people."

Turning away from her ex-lover's twisting body, Shanice chastised her hormones and refocused her attention on the faux fern.

"These plants are only temporary," Renee said as she handed over a beige folder. "After the gospel tour, this place is getting a complete makeover."

The handwriting on the one-page application had plenty of decorative loops. Shanice brightened. Lisa Whitmore left the employment section blank, but she was using a PO box as an address and she listed more than one phone number.

"I still don't understand," Shanice said. "How did you end up introducing her to Ms. Barbara?"

"Part of my program is to give students an opportunity to accompany me in a performance and sing background vocals. It gives them a chance to add a professional experience to their portfolio."

"You get people to pay you for the privilege of singing behind you?"

"Lisa and Tiana Sands, another student, were supposed to perform with me at the Black Moses event. Tiana backed out at the last minute. I don't do duets but decided to let Lisa come to the event as my guest. So we're schmoozing the crowd, I'm introducing her to local politicians, museum patrons, socialites, etc. When the program began, I took my place at the podium to sing 'How Great Thou Art.' The lights dimmed, all eyes were on me – except Barbara and Lisa. There were off in a corner whispering to each other."

"Instant friendship," Shanice said.

Renee rolled her eyes. "Afterward, all Lisa could talk about was how Barbara was going to help her get a grant for something or another. I told her that Barbara was long on promises and short on follow through. Lisa didn't like me talking bad about her new best friend."

"You haven't seen her since then?"

"For the next month, she was here promptly on Thursdays at 7 p.m. for her lesson. Then suddenly, she stopped coming. The phone numbers she put on her application were out of service. I sent a flier to her PO box and it came back with no forwarding address."

No longer convinced of its value, Shanice folded the application into a neat square and shoved it into her back pocket. "You have no idea why she stopped coming?"

"In a pay-as-you-go situation, some students are bound to be flaky. Honestly, I didn't even know she and Barbara were still in contact with each other." Renee looked at her watch. "I have a client due in fifteen minutes and I'd like to freshen up before she gets here. Make sure you tell Walter I tried to help. Things are starting to come together for me and I can't afford to have him believe that I'd do anything to actually harm them."

"Sure." Shanice got up. "Whatever happened to your sister and StoneTalker?"

"Renita got tired of both him and her husband. She's in Aruba with Jerry, her optometrist."

"What?"

"Yeah, girl. Trust me, nobody saw that coming."

As Shanice stepped off of the elevator, Detective Gerard came out of the coffee shop. "Ms. Wilkins," he said. "This is a surprise." He tossed his cup in the trash and beckoned her over. "What are you doing here?"

"Visiting a friend."

"What's this friend's name?"

"Renee."

"Renee Jordan? That's interesting."

Before he could probe deeper, Shanice volunteered more info. "She's the friend who recommended me to the church."

"When I interviewed you," Gerard consulted his notes, "you referred to Ms. Jordan as a client. Now she's a friend? Ok." He scribbled in his book. "It's my understanding that Ms. Jordan and Barbara Robinson had a falling out."

"I don't know anything about that."

"Has Pastor Robinson been giving her private sermons?"

Though disgusted by his innuendo, Shanice was relieved that Renee's secret was intact. She shook her head. "I don't know her personal business like that, but I can't imagine them being more than acquaintances."

"I know it's distasteful, but think about it. What's their body language like when they are together?"

Shanice kept her voice even, but she was furious. The detective was trying to catch her in a lie. "I've never been in the same room with them. Remember, I only recently met Pastor Robinson."

"Are you sure, Ms. Wilkins? I don't want you to go home, suddenly remember something, and relay the message through Officer Childress."

"The pictures." Shanice closed her eyes and sighed.

Gerard slapped the notebook against his open palm. "I told you to contact me directly. This is my investigation." His raised voice turned a few heads, but no one dared challenge him.

"I was tired," Shanice said. "I didn't feel like--"

He scoffed. "You didn't feel like being inconvenienced? Barbara Robinson is in the morgue; she doesn't feel anything."

"I am sorry. I wanted to get as far away from death as possible. It was overwhelming."

Gerard leaned in so close, she could see remnants of whipped cream in his mustache. "I don't like lies or sins of omission," he said. "Is there anything you need to tell me?"

Shanice knew that if he sensed uncertainty or fear in her response, he would continue pecking away at her. Holding his gaze, she answered. "No."

The detective grunted before turning his back on her and walking toward the elevator. "Good afternoon, Ms. Wilkins. Let's not run into each other again."

Chapter 12

Debra confidently strode down the street with a hefty, eco-friendly shopping bag. She loved working at The Chopin Cart, a gourmet grocery store that catered to shoppers' high-end tastes. It paid well, had great benefits, and her co-workers were decent. The customers, on the other hand, were less than ideal. They had come out in full force for Taleggio Tuesdays. After being trapped behind a windowless deli counter for eight hours, Debra finally was able to relax. The sunlight on her face felt wonderful.

When she first moved to Maynard, her shaved head and distinctive bop earned her a variety of stares. It wasn't until Jenkins and Adler began including her in their banter that she really felt at home. Their first interaction hinged on an inaccurate assumption.

"Hey, young blood." Jenkins had called out – summoning Debra over to the stoop.

She was ready for small talk, but Adler made it clear they had an agenda. "When you gonna do right by Gina and put a ring on her finger?"

"Huh?" Debra's confusion was evident.

Jenkins bristled. "That's the problem with young people; always wanting to play house. Gina isn't living in a dollhouse, boy. The time for games is over."

"Don't fret, son," Adler added. "We've seen you bringing groceries and stuff into the house. Unlike these deadbeats out here, you seem to be about something."

Debra looked down at her ensemble; her breasts were obvious even in the loose-fitting hoodie. "I'm not a dude," she said. By then, Adler and Jenkins were too far into their rant to hear anything she said.

"Half these young bucks leave high school with two or three baby mammas." Jenkins stomped to emphasize his point. "Glad I don't have any girls. I'd be in jail three times over for cracking knuckleheads' skulls."

"Gina got a good head on her shoulders, but a woman's heart was created to play the fool."

Debra straightened up – making sure the twins were front and center – and cleared her throat. "I'm not Gina's boyfriend. I'm not a guy."

The mouths of the older gentlemen slammed shut. Adler was the first to recover. "Well, it figures. Gina is Mavis' niece; they are both fruits of the same tree."

Jenkins scoffed. "That don't make one bit of difference. Y'all can get married. I keep up with the news."

Debra could have clarified further – but if they believed she was Gina's girlfriend instead of a tenant, it wasn't her fault.

Since then, most residents acknowledged her presence. Guys who couldn't bring themselves to speak graced her with a curt nod as they passed.

Ladies who hadn't kept up with local gossip were usually enlightened when an attempt at flirting went awry. After the initial eye contact had been made, the woman would let her gaze wander from Debra's handsomely boyish face downward – stopping abruptly at the chest. After a double take, she would quickly look away, embarrassed.

Debra loved watching straight women get flustered. It made up for her confusing teen years. Back then, she fell in love with any girl who looked in her direction. Each flutter of the heart brought an infusion of excitement and sheer terror.

By sophomore year of college, the tables had turned. Debra was out, open, and secure. From Macroeconomics to Digital Film Making, she flirted with all her female classmates. Sometimes, Debra found herself trading innuendo with a woman who called her bluff. That was when the game really got interesting. Thankfully, she never ran afoul of a pissed-off boyfriend.

Turning the corner, Debra caught a glimpse of a brown-skinned woman in a canary yellow dress behind her. As the cadence of high heels striking the pavement drew closer, she moved over to allow her fellow pedestrian to pass. Rather than taking the chance to launch ahead, the woman slowed down.

Maybe I should introduce myself, Debra thought. A sharp pain in her left ankle made her yelp. Not paying attention, she had stepped awkwardly on uneven pavement. She felt herself losing her balance, but a hand caught her arm and helped steady her.

"Are you okay?" her rescuer asked. Though petite, the canary woman had an iron grip.

Debra nodded, even though the near fall left her light-headed. "Yeah, thanks." Feeling a bit silly, she couldn't stop herself from over-explaining. "I'm always daydreaming and tripping over myself, but there's not always a beautiful angel to catch me."

The canary's look of concern gave way to a bright smile. "How would you like a chance to help out a damsel in distress?"

Debra did a faux bow. "You saved my ankle; I at least owe you a favor. I'm Debra. What can I do for you?"

The woman retrieved a business card from her shoulder bag. "My name is Cynthia Tavares and I'm a graduate student at Byrne. My master's thesis is on the ramifications of successful community challenges to urban renewal projects in Ardola."

"Really? That sounds…"

"Boring as hell. I have opinions on the legal rulings, plenty of charts and graphs illustrating economic trends and crime, etc. What I'm missing is actual insight from the people most affected by the outcome. I've been canvassing the neighborhood, hoping to find a few people to agree to interviews. Debra, do you live in Maynard?"

"Yeah, a few houses down the block." They began walking again. "I don't think interviewing me would help much. There's lots of older people who remember."

Cynthia threw up a hand and the bracelets adorning her wrist jangled erratically. "The two older gentlemen across the street spent nearly forty-five minutes detailing many of Maynard's heroic battles against the city. Now I'm interested in the perspectives of other residents, their outlook on the community, and what they see for the future."

"Sorry, I'm still not what you're looking for. I've only been here a year." Seeing disappointment in Cynthia's eyes, Debra backtracked quickly. "What you need to do is talk to Gina Smallwood, my landlord. She inherited our house – her house – from a great aunt a few years ago." She checked her watch. "Why don't you come inside? Gina will be home in a few minutes."

"Sure."

Debra whispered a brief prayer before unlocking the door. A quick look around the living room and her worries disappeared. The pillows on the sofa needed to be rearranged, but there was no half-dressed web designer lying about. To make sure, she called out. "Shanice? You decent? I've got company." When there was no response, she stepped aside and, with a flourish, waved Cynthia inside. "Please make yourself at home."

Walking in slowly, Cynthia carefully took in every detail of the room. She dropped her purse on the sofa. "I thought your landlord's name was Gina."

"Shanice is our other housemate."

Debra went into the kitchen, tossed her dirty apron down the basement stairs, and hastily put the shopping bag directly in the fridge. There would be plenty of time to properly put away groceries later.

"Would you like something to drink?"

"A glass of water would be nice."

There were only six ice cubes left in the freezer, so Debra

put all of them in the glass designated for her guest and poured bottled water for them both. Returning to the living room, she found Cynthia looking at the photos on the mantel of the faux fireplace.

"You go to Warner?" the visitor asked as she inspected a photograph of Debra and friends in front of the school library.

"Not anymore," Debra said. "School was a blessing and a curse. I was happy to get away from home, but not ready to spend four more years in class for a business degree I didn't really want. Decided to get a job instead."

"Why not find another major?"

"I needed a little breathing room to figure everything out. I don't regret the time I spent there – met some great people. I'm not ready to settle down into a career." They exchanged sly smiles. "Tell me about you. How did you get interested in urban planning?"

"When I graduated from high school, I had visions of moving to New York and becoming an actress. I enrolled in a theater program, confident that the professors would think I was the most talented thing ever. I had my headshots; I was ready to get in front of a camera."

"Didn't work out that way, huh?"

"I didn't expect to start off in lead roles, but most of those directors weren't looking for someone with my aesthetic. When I did go to auditions, hundreds of other women showed up too. That didn't suit me at all; I want a career where employers compete for my attention."

The front door opened and a tired Gina walked in on stockinged feet, shoes in hand. She smiled politely at the stranger, but it wasn't the first time she had come home to find Debra entertaining company. Her plan to slip by was thwarted when the guest jumped up and offered her hand.

"Hi, I'm Cynthia. You must be Shanice."

Gina tucked her shoes under her arm and reluctantly accepted the invitation to shake hands. "Actually, I'm Gina."

"I'm sorry, Ms. Smallwood. You look good for your

age."

"Excuse me?" Gina looked past Cynthia to Debra, who had pulled a pillow over her face to conceal her laughter.

Chapter 13

Despite signs with conflicting parking regulations, Shanice was able to find a space directly across the street from the storefront church. A light was on inside, but she didn't feel particularly hopeful. It had been a long, fruitless day.

After a better night's sleep, she had plunged head first into Project Find Lisa. Unable to find any new information with the disconnected phone numbers, she focused on the church affiliation part of application. The mystery woman had claimed membership in New Life.

There were eight churches in the city with New Life in the title and Shanice had used up a considerable amount of gas chasing a phantom. A fire, kindled by lightning, had gutted out New Life in the Redeemer. New Life in Christ turned out to be little more than a sign in a grimy basement window. Though no one had thought to update its website, New Life Baptist had changed its name to Nu Lyfe.

Now, scoping out her fourth house of worship, Shanice wondered if "New Life" was a red herring.

Then, a woman wearing a wide-brimmed hat and an ankle-length skirt rounded the corner and went into the building. Putting her doubts aside, Shanice fished a few quarters from the ashtray and bought an hour on the meter. Looking around the sanctuary couldn't hurt and finding something interesting could give her the illusion of progress.

The dank entryway was barely lit. A hand-drawn thermometer showed how far the congregation had come in raising $150K for the building fund. They still had $105K to go. In the actual sanctuary, big hat and several other women set up folding chairs and prepared the altar. As her gaze swept over a small table, a flier with a familiar rainbow caught her attention. It was for a fashion show to spotlight local designers and raise money for the upcoming Black Pride.

In her peripheral vision, Shanice saw an orange dot moving toward her. When she turned, the dot turned out to be a woman wearing a skin-tight neon orange dress with lime green accessories. "Good evening, I'm Sister Charlene. May I help you?"

In the car, Shanice had prepared a few stories to explain why she was looking for Lisa. In her imagination, the scenarios played out perfectly. Confronted with speaking to a real person, the practiced lies felt inadequate. None of the stories she crafted made sense. She improvised. "A friend is a member here and she really raves about the church, so I decided to check it out."

"What's your friend's name?"

"I'm not sure. Actually, we met at a club . . ." Shanice tried to maintain eye contact but lying didn't come easy.

Charlene laughed. "Lust may have brought you here, but love will make you stay!"

Looking down at her jeans, Shanice took a step back. "I'm not dressed for service."

"Dress codes come from man, not God. All He sees is your heart. Follow me."

Shanice did as she was told. She got an earful about the history of New Life Sanctuary and was introduced to each member of the set-up crew. The other women acknowledged them and continued setting up. After Charlene recounted her own fall from grace and return to redemption, she launched into a full-blown testimony. "They tried to separate me from my faith, but – Hallelujah! – God brought me back! They tried to kill my spirit and condemn me to hell. They called themselves Christians, but they don't know my God!"

Big hat came to the rescue. "Charlene, do we have juice for the refreshment table?"

The authoritarian voice was enough to snap Charlene from her holy trance. "Juice! I'm on it, Sister Luanda. I was on my way to the store for cranberry juice." She turned to Shanice. "What's your name, honey?"

"Janice," Shanice lied.

"Janice, hope you stick around for Prayer Power Hour." Charlene gave her arm a firm squeeze before sauntering down the newly created center-aisle.

Conscious of the eyes of the other women upon her, Shanice asked for the ladies' room and was directed to a small alcove separated from the sanctuary by a curtain. She splashed water on her face and took a moment to regroup. *There has to be an easier way to do this,* she thought.

Next to the bathroom was a bulletin board with pictures from a recent women's day celebration. It dawned on Shanice that Lisa could be one of the many faces staring back at her. She took the photo of Lisa from her jacket pocket and scanned the wall for a match.

The women were a beautiful rainbow of hues, shapes, and sizes. They were all decked out in a combination of white and gold, but Charlene stood out with her glittery golden beehive. Lisa was nowhere to be found.

Feeling the beginning of a headache coming on, Shanice closed her eyes. It was time to go home. Maybe she'd check out the remaining churches tomorrow – if the rising feeling of disappointment could be tamed.

A flurry of voices echoed through the building. Peeking into the sanctuary, Shanice saw parishioners arriving and greeting each other. Among those exchanging hugs and kisses of welcome was a familiar face. A gray utilitarian blouse hid her toned arms and bobby pins corralled her curly tendrils into a bun. Shanice had no doubt the woman being greeted was Barbara's dinner companion.

Shanice whispered, "Hallelujah!" and vowed to put a dollar in the offering plate.

Debra stood in the doorway watching Cynthia rush down the street, her bracelets playing a disjointed symphony. After the yellow blur disappeared, she went into the kitchen.

Gina had traded her stockings for slippers and was filling the empty ice trays. "I'm tired of coming home and having one of your friends give me the stink eye. How is this woman going to sit on my sofa and insult me?"

Debra took the grocery bag from the refrigerator and began putting canned goods and deli meats away. "Cynthia is not my friend, yet; we met a few minutes ago. She wasn't trying to be shady; she assumed a landlord would be more, um, advanced in age."

As soon as the path to the refrigerator was free, Gina grabbed a fruit cup and sat at the kitchen table. "You live with a sexy woman – two when Shanice gets into her GQ mode. It's a fact your girlfriends just need to deal with. They need to stop treating me like I'm the competition."

"You're exaggerating."

"Every time I cross Jelisa's path, she huffs and rolls her eyes like a toddler. If I say more than two words to you in Monica's presence, her rude ass pulls you away mid-conversation for kiss. You love it when these women act a fool over you."

Debra filled the bowl in the middle of the table with a just-arrived-off-the-truck-that-morning batch of handpicked organic mixed nuts. What was the use of working at an upscale store if you couldn't bring home upscale treats? "I'm honest about my intentions. I warn everyone that I'm not looking for anything serious." She smiled softly and batted her eyelashes, her face a vision of innocence. "If a woman is intimidated by our friendship, isn't it proof she's not the one?"

Playfully, Gina tapped the back of her spoon against Debra's nose. "Yet, somehow, you keep attracting the possessive, borderline obsessive ones. You don't see that as a problem?"

"Nope." Debra took the spoon away but held on to Gina's hand, gently caressing her fingers. "My problem is the woman I'm chasing after won't let me catch her."

"Oh, sweetheart," Gina said as she retracted her hand, "it's because she knows you're not looking for anything serious." She tossed the empty container into the garbage can and left.

Debra wanted to kick herself. The tongue that talked her into others' sheets always betrayed her in front of the woman she wanted. She found Gina in the living room. "Anyway, I only invited Cynthia in to talk to you. She's doing some project on urban renewal."

"That's why she scampered away as soon as I got home?"

"She bolted because you hit her with the icy stare of doom." Debra felt the business card in her pocket. "I may have to call the poor thing to make sure she isn't traumatized."

When Gina straightened the pillows on the sofa, a glint of yellow caught her eye. Fingers cautiously exploring the crevice between cushions, she struck gold – a gold butterfly earring with emerald wings nestled in its post. It disappeared into her fist. "No," she said. "We haven't seen the last of Ms. Tavares."

Elder Vera adjusted her black pillbox hat, clutched the microphone stand for support, and began praying. Ten minutes later, it looked like she had finally run out of things to be thankful for. Then she got a second wind. "And, Lord, we want to thank you for the honey bee . . ."

Folding chairs were not built for epic prayers and pain crept slowly up Shanice's back. When she lifted her head prematurely, an usher glared at her. Sighing, she went back to staring at the scuffed tiled floor. The church was only half filled, but she sat in the back. Everyone she encountered so far had been as welcoming – though not as chatty – as Charlene.

A loud amen reverberated throughout the room. Charlene plopped down in the seat next to her. Someone began singing; they had to get close to talk. "Enjoying the service so far?" she whispered.

"I'm not sure my neck can handle it." Charlene giggled, attracting the attention of the now scowling usher. Shanice shushed her. "Be careful, you're going to get us thrown out of here."

Charlene discreetly unwrapped a peppermint. "Don't pay Tisha no mind. We don't. Are you still looking for Ms. Right?"

Shanice pointed to the mystery woman. "I think she's in the second row, third seat from the left. Hard to tell without a cloud of smoke between us."

"So Lisa is your type?" Charlene's lashes fluttered away her disappointment.

"Lisa?" Shanice repeated.

"Her real name is Nicole, but she prefers her middle name – Lisa. You didn't meet her at a club, though. She's too afraid that she'll run into a parent and put her job in jeopardy."

Suddenly, the entire congregation was on its feet. "What's happening? Another offering?" Shanice began patting her pockets for loose change.

"No, it's altar call." Shanice's blank expression prompted Charlene to continue. "If a person wants to, they can walk up to the altar and Sister Verna and Brother Paul will do an actual laying of hands on them."

Tears streaming down her face, Lisa stepped out of her row and approached the altar. Once there, she lowered herself into the waiting arms of Sister Verna. Laying a hand on the back of her neck, Brother Paul took the microphone. "Lord, we ask that you give Sister Lisa strength. Whispering voices are pulling her hither and yon. She needs you to shine a light on her path. Father, show her your will; show her your way."

Was she seeking comfort or forgiveness? Shanice thought.

Though she had a handful of tattered tissues, rivers of tears flowed freely down Lisa's cheeks. Two other women joined hands with Sister Verna to form a ring of protection around her.

Ten minutes later, there was a quick prayer for safe journeys and the service was over. Several people crowded around Lisa, offering encouragement. Charlene tugged Shanice's hand. "Come on; I'll introduce you to her."

Shanice pulled back. This wasn't the time or the place for the conversation she wanted to have. "It looks like she needs her friends right now."

Charlene worked her way to the front to share her own words of comfort. Pointing at Shanice, she whispered to Lisa, whose eyes filled with fear. Others at the front turned to find out what upset their friend.

Shanice suddenly felt exposed. She quickly joined the small procession heading out the door.

Pausing to rip a flier off the windshield, Shanice pulled off as Charlene's anklet-adorned foot stepped onto the sidewalk.

Chapter 14

The next morning, Shanice woke up to the smell of bacon wafting into her room. She groaned and retreated under the covers. The last time this happened, she rushed down to the kitchen and ran smack into disappointment. Turned out her bedroom window was open; the aroma had drifted over from Mrs. Barton's next door.

One thing she missed about home was breakfast. Even when her mom was baking chicken tenders rolled in yogurt and cornflakes as a substitute for frying, she still made pancakes, French toast, bacon, and biscuits oozing with butter.

Sitting up, Shanice realized her window was not open. That tantalizing aroma was coming from inside the house!

She grabbed a pair of sweatpants from the foot of the bed and clambered down the steps. When she first moved in, she wouldn't dare leave her room without being showered and dressed for the day. That ended the day she walked in on Gina in the living room, nonchalantly taking a nap with a mango mud-mask hardening on her face. They'd seen each other in various stages of undress and hygiene since then.

Walking into the kitchen, she witnessed Gina transferring bacon from a frying pan to a plate that was already piled high.

Debra was leaning against the counter, grasping a coffee mug with both hands. "Damn," she said. "You couldn't have stayed in bed for two more minutes?"

Shanice raised her eyebrows. "If you only need two

minutes, it's probably not something worth doing." She went straight to the coffeemaker and made a show of turning her back to them. "Just pretend I'm not here."

Gina laughed. "Deb's mad because she lost the bet. I knew you'd be here before I finished cooking, but she swore that nothing short of a miracle would get you out of bed before eight." She sat at the kitchen table and patted the seat next to her. "Come. Now Deb has to serve us and clean up."

"Sorry," Shanice said. A plate of orange juice, bacon, and boiled eggs was set before her.

"You've slept through fire alarms," Debra said. "Why are you awake now?"

"Because food is life. What would you have won if I hadn't made it?"

"We would have gotten a nice hot breakfast tomorrow too. I was looking out for both of us." Debra slapped the back of Shanice's neck with a damp dishtowel before taking her own seat.

After having a second helping of bacon, Shanice realized Gina was fully dressed and accessorized. "What inspired this?" She waved a fork over her almost empty plate.

"I have to be in Althea's chair at nine and the only decent takeout spot near her shop doesn't open until eleven." Getting to work at nine might be a challenge for Gina, but she was never late for a hair appointment. "I could have cooked enough for myself, but that would have been cruel."

"Speaking of cruelty," Debra said, "I called Cynthia to apologize for your behavior."

"Excuse me?"

"Just kidding. I let her know we found her earring. She's ashamed of the way things went yesterday and wants to apologize to you directly."

Shanice tapped her juice glass to remind her roommates they weren't alone. "What happened?"

Gina rolled her eyes. "No need for apologies. I'm over it."

Shanice tried again. "Is this a new girlfriend?"

"Not yet,' Debra admitted, "but I'm working on that. I inadvertently invited her over for dinner."

"What are you making?" Gina asked. She finished her coffee. "I know you aren't expecting me to feed your date."

"It's not a date and there won't ever be one if I go near a stove."

After delicately dabbing the corners of her mouth with a napkin, Gina retouched her lipstick. "You spend eight hours a day around food; you'll figure something out." She patted Debra's shoulder on the way out. "The first step is doing the dishes. Have a good day, ladies."

Debra pushed her plate away and Shanice helped herself to a barely nibbled piece of rye toast. "You met Cynthia at Sapphic Sunday?"

"On the sidewalk."

"A neighborhood girl? That's new."

"I don't know where she lives, but it's not here. I was in the right place at the right time." Debra began stacking dirty plates. "What's new with you?"

Shanice shrugged. *Not this time,* she thought. *There's no way I'm telling you anything that could come back to haunt me.* "It's a beautiful day. I'll see where it goes."

Chapter 15

Gina relaxed as warm water and gentle fingers massaged her scalp. Hands directed the flow away from her eyes while squeezing the remaining shampoo out of her hair. Softness brushed against her cheek and she opened her eyes to see Alma's bosom swaying over her. It would have sent a flirtatious rush through her body if Alma weren't her second cousin.

The shop had filled up in the few minutes she had been at the sink. Most of the people there were relatives. When first cousin Althea opened Crimps & Curls, she didn't have a problem with offering immediate family a fifteen percent discount for their patronage. Word spread quickly to cousins who thought the bloodline, no matter how diluted, entitled them to savings. She had to put a stop to it when her mother's "church family" thought they qualified for the same deal.

Now Althea set aside three days a year to give family a discount of twenty-five percent. It was a great way to keep in contact with female relatives and Cousin William, the only boy in the family with a full-on perm.

Between blasts of water, Gina heard snatches of conversation. "Althea, when are you going to put a flat screen in here? I'm tired of squinting my eyes at that little television." That was Aunt Gloria. "Might as well turn it off; can't hear a thing on it anyway."

"I'll take it into consideration." Althea's voice was flat. That was the one drawback of having family as customers: they figured they were doing you a favor, so they got to give unsolicited advice.

A chorus of chatter broke out after that, but a strong voice rose above the din. "Gloria, ya can't see what's on TV if your nose is stuck in somebody else's business." Ella, Gina's mother, had been antagonizing her older sister since the two shared a crib.

"Gloria, Ella – you two cut it out now." That was Grandma Wilma. "I can't put you over my knee anymore, but this cane can tap you."

After another round of lathering and rinsing, Alma pronounced her hair clean. Holding a towel around her head, Gina dutifully kissed each older relative on the cheek.

Grandma Wilma said, "Hey, baby. It's so good to see you. We were wondering about what you'd been up to."

Aunt Gloria cut her eyes at Gina. "Your hair ain't longer than that," she said, snapping her fingers. "Don't know why you wasting money getting it done. Now that you've got paying tenants, I guess you've got money to burn."

Gina routinely ignored verbal jabs from loved ones. The family was shocked when Great Aunt Mavis left her the house. Her mother, Grandma Wilma, and Aunt Gloria assumed the house would be sold and money divided amongst the survivors. When they came to her with a list of items that they wanted to claim before the sale, she thanked them for their help in planning the funeral and announced her plan to move in.

After getting over the shock that she would be getting neither the silver tea set nor a check, Aunt Gloria decided that her recently divorced daughter, Jamie, should be allowed to move in too. Gina torpedoed that plan in favor of non-thieving, paying tenants. Her aunt was still bitter.

Ella came to her daughter's defense. "Leave my baby alone. She didn't need Jamie eating up her food and running up her bills."

"Mmmmhmmm." Althea nodded firmly. The one time Jamie came to Family Day, she slipped out without paying.

Aunt Gloria folded her arms. "You not supposed to treat

family that way."

"But *Jamie's* your child," Ella countered. "If her husband don't want her, she goes back to you."

Grandma Wilma cleared her throat. "Gina, when you going to give me some great-grands? You need to find yourself a good man, a good husband." Aunt Gloria and Ella gave each other the look.

"I haven't met the right person yet," Gina said.

Alma came to the rescue. "Come on, Grandma, it's your turn at the sink."

Grandma Wilma carefully folded a page in her tattered *Jet* magazine before handing it over to Aunt Gloria. "Hold on to this. I want to finish reading it while I'm under the dryer." She hoisted herself up, grabbed her cane, and started toward the back of the salon. "Now, I got a lot of bobby pins in my hair. I want you to give me all of them back too. They are my lucky pins. Can't win bingo without them."

"Pay her no mind, honey," Ella said. She reached out to touch Gina's hand. "Momma forgets sometimes, that's all."

Aunt Gloria disagreed. "That woman doesn't forget; she just pretends to. Just like when everyone knew that Aunt Mavis and her friend were more than roommates."

Gina took Grandma Wilma's chair, searched the crowded magazine rack for current issues, and tried to hide her annoyance. Everyone in the family had been briefed on her sexual orientation. Cousin William had seen to that. Hours after he peeked through his bangs and saw her dancing at the Allegro, her parents wanted to have a frank discussion about her lifestyle.

Ella had the hardest time with it. A fan of true crime shows, she had always worried that Gina would go on a blind date with a young man who would dismember her. The "lesbian issue" opened a whole new dimension of fear. "It's like, my mind is replaying every slur I've heard in my life," she had said through tears. "Now I know those people were talking about my baby." To calm her mother's fears, Gina called two or three times a week.

Always ten minutes late to a conversation, Cousin Pam announced, "Aunt Gloria is on the right track, but this shop needs a total makeover. I have a more spiritual vision for it." She stretched out one hand toward the manicurist while the other toyed with the lavender crystal hanging around her neck. "What you need to do is get rid of all of these chemicals and run a full service natural salon." She paused to pick out the color and design she wanted for her nails.

As Althea began waving a hot curling iron at her latest critic, Aunt Gloria pointed to the television screen. "Look!" A picture of Jeff Conley appeared behind two somber newscasters.

Alma turned up the volume. "The coroner has determined that Hollywood insider Jeff Conley's death was accidental. The film producer had a mixture of alcohol and barbiturates in his bloodstream when he fell from the second floor balcony and struck his head before drowning in his swimming pool. The injury rendered him unconscious and he drowned." A montage of the blond, middle-aged Adonis posing with various celebrities filled the screen. "He is survived by his wife, Leila Conley, and his mother, Carmen Wolff."

Ella scoffed. "At first, they tried to blame an intruder, then his wife. Who knows what the truth is? They get up to all kinds of hell inside Milan Park."

The television blared. "We've got to take back our neighborhood," a brown-suited, white-haired black man was yelling to an assembled crowd.

The male news anchor explained, "Hope Reborn Baptist Church is holding a rally to, in the words of Deacon Jefferson Murphy, 'protest the violence that has encroached upon our lives.' The body of Mrs. Barbara Robinson – wife of Pastor Walter Robinson – was found in a classroom before Sunday school. The police are following up on several leads and have questioned a person of interest."

"Shame on Deacon Murphy," Aunt Gloria said. "Last week, he wouldn't even bother speaking to the people in the neighborhood." She softened her voice and leaned forward. "He's not much better with the members. If you're not important enough, he might nod but won't waste the energy to crack a smile."

Gina had been trying to tune her folks out, but now she wanted to hear everything. "You still go to Hope Reborn?"

Aunt Gloria looked a little uncomfortable "Only on the important days, Easter and New Year's Eve."

"We stopped going when they added a fourth offering," Pam cut in. "Then we started going to New Mount Carmel, but that place turned out to be a worse drain on the pocketbook." Her hands fluttered wildly, but she was still careful not to smudge her fresh manicure. "Rev. Ralph always has a new project in need of immediate funding: the elevator fund, pastors' aid fund, build a church in Africa. A lot of people at New Mount Carmel can barely keep body and soul together – and Ralph collecting money for Africa?"

"Wow," Gina said.

Pam sucked her teeth. "He was one of the ministers profiled in Ceeda Truth's 'Thieves in the Temple' column. She didn't name names, of course, but everyone knows he is the one who went to South Africa to build a church and came back with nothing but pictures of himself on safari."

Now that she had dropped that financial bombshell, Pam was ready to relinquish the stage. "It is a shame about Mrs. Robinson, though. Who's going to the funeral?"

Aunt Gloria frowned. "Don't know if I want to. Fast living is catching up to the people Paul and I used to run around with. Feels like every other month we are staring at somebody in a coffin. And the way they said Barbara was busted up...I need a break from death."

Ella held a magazine up to her lips, as if to whisper. "They say Robinson was with one of his women when he found his wife."

"What!" Gina was too shocked to be embarrassed by her outburst.

"They were planning to," her mother paused to find the

right words, "get intimate before service."

Aunt Gloria shook her head vigorously. "No, it was nothing like that at all. It was some fast-tail little girl that needed info about that teen pregnancy program Barbara was involved in."

Ella shrugged. "It's what I heard. Rumors always have him sneaking women in and out of his bedroom."

"Oh, he's a dog like the rest of them," Aunt Gloria said. "He doesn't do his dirt in church, though. Remember when Barbara moved out to take care of her sick friend? Pastor Walter's women were getting on her nerves."

Althea motioned for Gina to sit in her chair. Removing the towel, the stylist ran her fingers through the damp tresses. "Girl, I'm going to give you a hot oil treatment. Whatever holding spray you use is stripping the life out of your hair."

Reluctantly, Gina allowed herself to be led to the back of the salon. Aunt Gloria's voice was the last one she heard before going under the dryer. "It was a miserable marriage; they weren't fooling anybody."

Chapter 16

Thanks to Charlene, Shanice had enough information to refocus her online investigation. If Lisa, aka Nicole, needed to keep her life carefully hidden, she was probably a teacher at a private school. A few clicks later, the faculty profile page of Nicole L. Whitmore, a math teacher at St. James Elementary School, filled her screen. A graduate of the University of Nebraska, she had been tormenting third and fourth graders for only two years.

Shanice decided to pay the teacher a visit. Going for a PTA-ready mom look, she waded through her closet to find the clothes her mother had gotten her for Christmas. In shapeless black jeans and a turquoise tunic, she looked like she had stepped out of the pages of a J.C. Penney catalog.

Located off a major thoroughfare, St. James Elementary School had heavy traffic leading up to its doors. Shanice could only imagine what it was like at the start of the school day with yellow busses and helicopter parents competing for the same two lanes.

Walking into the school, Shanice heard children's voices echoing in the empty hallway. No one was at the security desk, so she continued toward the main office. Though the door was closed, shadows moved beyond the frosted glass. A few steps beyond the checkpoint was a bronze plaque that bore the image of barefoot St. James and a prayer: *Lord, unworthy of the grace you have bestowed upon us, we pledge ourselves to thee. We humbly submit to thine will. We pray that through us, others will experience your wonder, power, and glory. Through us may your light shine.* It struck her as an unfair burden to put on people before they hit puberty.

When the security guard returned to his post, he was startled to see Shanice in the corridor. "What are you doing here?" He pointed at the desk. "Visitors are supposed to stop there until being given permission to go further." The elderly black man could barely squeeze into his uniform, but the brass nameplate bearing his name – A. Cartwright – sparkled.

Shanice followed him back to the vestibule. "I'm sorry, but there was no one here and I thought –"

He sneered and pointed to a handwritten sign advising visitors to wait for security. "Can't you read? We don't allow anyone to just walk in from off the street."

"This is the way you speak to parents?" Shanice didn't yell, but she made sure her voice carried.

The guard was confused. "I've never seen you here before; you aren't one of our parents."

"I wanted to get information about the school. If I'm undesirable, I can't imagine my child will be welcomed here."

That caught the attention of the figures behind the glass. The door opened and a silver-haired white woman peeked out. "Anthony, is everything all right out here?"

Cartwright smiled and the edge left his voice. "Everything is fine, Mrs. Grant. It's a small misunderstanding. Ma'am, can I see a photo ID, please?" His feet shifted when Shanice produced a license. "Please continue to the main office; Mrs. Grant can answer any questions you have about the school."

Shanice made sure he saw the malice in her eyes. "Thank you, Anthony."

In the office, a full-sized portrait of St. James grasping a sword on horseback glowered at all who entered. At the bidding of the older woman, Shanice signed the registry. "I'm Julia Grant, one of the administrators. How can I help you," she turned the book around, "Mrs. Wilkins?"

"Ms. Wilkins."

Mrs. Grant's lips disappeared into a tight line. "At St. James, we provide an atmosphere conducive to learning while not neglecting children's moral growth. I don't mean to be insensitive, but we believe that solid moral grounding starts with a traditional, two-parent family."

Shanice knew the school policy and was prepared. "My nephew had that before my sister and brother-in-law were killed by a drunk driver last year." Mrs. Grant made the appropriate sympathetic groan. "I thought dealing with their deaths and the chaos of public school would be a bit much for Jackson, but I've never heard of a Christian theology that assumes orphans are morally inferior."

Mrs. Grant was horrified. "That's not what we teach at all. We take pride in addressing our students' spiritual needs. We need to make sure children aren't exposed to ideas about family that aren't Bible-based. Jackson would find comfort here."

Shanice folded her arms; the school wasn't off the hook yet. "The security here is pretty aggressive. Do you have a problem with strangers trying to get in?"

"Oh, no. Anthony loves the school and is a little overzealous." Mrs. Grant forced a chuckle and cleared her throat. "Did someone recommend St. James?"

Shanice decided to take a gamble. "I've spoken to a teacher who touted St. James' academic program, so I thought I'd stop by to learn more. Her name was Nicole."

The administrator's face lit up and the crow's feet around her eyes turned intensified. "Nicole Whitmore! She's such a treasure. The students all love her and it's good to know that she sings our praises." She turned to a woman sitting behind a desk. "Lauren, can you ask Ms. Whitmore to stop by? She should be on her lunch break now."

The secretary switched on the intercom. "Ms. Whitmore to the main office."

"Oh, I didn't want to disturb her." *At least not now,* Shanice thought. This wasn't time for a confrontation.

Lisa entered from a door in the back and stopped short

when she saw who was waiting for her. "I'm sorry," Shanice said. "I only wanted to pick up a brochure. I didn't want to interrupt your day."

Mrs. Grant waved dismissively. "A quick tour from someone you already know is better. I'm sure Ms. Whitmore won't mind."

Shanice shrugged apologetically while Lisa opened the door. "It's nice seeing you again," the teacher lied. "Let's start with the music department; it's right down the hall." Once away from the office, Lisa's face turned to stone. "You leave right now or I'm calling security."

"Listen, I don't know who you think I am, but I'm not here to threaten or harm you." Shanice kept her voice low. She didn't want round two with Anthony. "I just want to talk."

"I don't want to talk to you."

"Before Barbara Robinson died, she asked me to find you. I know she's gone, but I'm trying to keep my word."

"How do I know that I can trust you? Ellicott City?"

Shanice winced. "Okay, you know where my parents live."

"For Barbara?"

"Yes."

Lisa stared down at her sensible shoes. Then she sighed. "We've got a few minutes before the lunch period is over. Let's go to my classroom."

Chapter 17

Lisa held out half of a sandwich. "It's peanut butter and raspberry jam on whole wheat."

"No thanks." Shanice couldn't fold herself to fit into one of the student desks, so she leaned against a corkboard. "I'm disturbing you enough as it is."

"Was Barbara worried about me?" Lisa asked. "I miss her."

"In a way. She wanted me to find out if you were the one blackmailing her."

Lisa shook her head. "No, no, no! How could I?"

"Someone sent her pictures of the two of you together at the Bitmore."

"So?"

"They tried hard to suggest the images weren't innocent." Shanice showed her the picture and pointed out the closeness of Ms. Barbara's elbow. "To most people, it's two friends having fun at dinner. Whoever mailed this included a bible verse about abomination. The Robinsons thought you and Renee were working together. Renee denied everything. That leaves you."

"I'd never do anything to hurt Barbara. She wasn't a mentor; she was a friend. We confided in each other."

Shanice didn't relish sticking her finger in the wound, but she had to push back. "Come on; she didn't even know your real name."

Wrapping the remains of her sandwich in wax paper, Lisa pushed it into her lunch bag. She walked over to a window and watched a group of uniformed children playing dodge ball. When she spoke, her voice was barely above a whisper. "Do you know who Donna Sampson is?"

"Yeah," Shanice said. The name had come up several times during her online research of St. James Elementary. "That's the teacher who had an abortion and got fired."

"No. The abortion happened when she was a teenager. She got fired for admitting to it in an article about formerly wild teens who turned their lives around. A parent brought the piece to the school's attention and a thirty-two-year-old woman was terminated over a decision she made at fifteen."

"They actually fired someone over a seventeen-year-old sin?"

"God forgives. Parents at elite Christian institutions do not. That's why I've been determined to keep my private life separate from my work life. Peers and business professionals know me by Nicole, my first name. They have no idea what movies I like or what music I listen to. For acquaintances and friends, I use my middle name – Lisa – and don't go into detail about my job. I know it sounds weird, but I always feel like I need to keep a bit of myself in reserve."

"No, I get it."

Lisa fought back tears. "Barbara understood too. Initially, I didn't know she was a minister's wife. She liked our outings because she could be herself instead of First Lady of the Church."

"Whose idea was it to do the spa weekend?"

Lisa smiled. "Hers. You know, weekend getaway for the girls. We got massages, had a lavish lunch, and talked things out poolside. Like she and Dorothy used to."

Who is Dorothy? Shanice wanted to know but couldn't ask. Because she portrayed herself as a confidant of Barbara, Lisa expected her to know. She hoped the answer would present itself. "What did you talk about?"

"Our lives. What we wanted to do. She advised me to find a new job where I could feel confident being myself. Barbara had been able to pull off balancing a public persona with a personal life, but it wore on her. I'm not sure how she and Dorothy survived all those years. She couldn't live openly without jeopardizing the ministry."

Shanice joined her by the window. "What happened? Why did you disappear?"

"I started getting weird calls. I'd answer and the person would hang. Blocking the numbers didn't help. I didn't think anything of it at first. Then I left Renee's studio one day and there was a note on my car. 'I know what you're up to, bitch.'" The memory sent a shiver through Lisa. "I was terrified. I cut ties with everyone and took off sick for a few days."

"That's scary."

Lisa nodded. "I was holed up in the house, afraid to do anything. Days passed and nothing happened. I came back to work not knowing what to expect, but no one said anything out of the ordinary. I began to feel normal – until this strange woman showed up at my church and my job." She cracked a weary smile. "How did you find me?"

"It wasn't easy; I wasn't sure you actually existed. Eventually, I got your church affiliation from the application you filled out for Renee's lessons."

"Damn."

Shanice took an index card from the teacher's desk and wrote down her details. "I didn't mean to frighten you and I don't want to take up any more of your time. If you remember anything strange about the spa day or you need to talk, give me a call."

Lisa hesitated before taking the card and putting it in her pocket. "So Barbara died thinking that I betrayed her?" She pinched her eyes shut but couldn't stop the tears from flowing. "Please leave. I need a few minutes before my kids come back."

Shanice wanted to offer more than empty platitudes, but the words wouldn't come. She stepped out into the hallway and gently closed the door behind her.

Traffic ground to a halt to allow a procession of bulldozers to cross into a construction site and one of the machines promptly broke down. To pass the time, Shanice pulled out her notebook and tried reconstructing the timeline that led up to her meeting with the Robinsons. Someone had seen and photographed Lisa and Barbara at dinner. Then they harassed Lisa, who responded by disappearing. A few weeks later, the Robinsons received photographs in the mail.

A whole lot of the puzzle was still missing. Rather than being the key to the truth, finding Lisa only led to more questions.

The cell phone began gyrating in the passenger seat. A quick check on the traffic situation confirmed that she wasn't moving anytime soon, so Shanice answered it. Her greeting was met with belligerence and she cursed herself for not screening the call.

"That damned Detective Gerard has been to the studio and my apartment," Renee said. "He treated me like a suspect! I don't know what kind of games you and Walter are playing –"

"Why didn't you tell me about Barbara's lover?" Shanice asked.

And Renee shut right up.

Chapter 18

How had she and Dorothy survived all those years?

Lisa confirmed something that Shanice had started to suspect: Pastor Robinson wasn't the only one with a girlfriend. Why would Ms. Barbara be worried about the false narrative in the photographs, unless the underlying suggestion was true?

It was a secret that she had successfully kept hidden from the world. No one would believe that the righteous prude she portrayed had any carnal desires. Rumors about her sexuality would prompt laughter, not suspicion.

Pastor Robinson had to know. Their marriage of convenience gave cover to his philandering and shielded her from speculation. That was why Ms. Barbara didn't worry about his affairs and he insisted on silencing any lesbian rumors before they started.

When Renee recovered her voice, she was furious. "Where are you? Why are you discussing this out in public?"

"I'm in my car." Shanice again surveyed the chaotic scene around her. "Nobody can hear me."

Renee wasn't convinced. "I hear horns and people yelling. If I can hear them, they can hear you!"

"Fine, I'm sorry. We need to talk about this, though. Meet you at the studio?"

"No. I'm hungry."

An hour later, they were in The Grey Pamplemousse, navigating the over-sized, laminated menus. The waiter introduced himself as Curtis and recited the daily specials as he quickly placed paper mats, silverware, and water on their table. "Are you two angels ready or do you need a few more minutes?" Not a hair in his faded orange shag shifted out of place.

"Chicken salad with bacon on rye for me," Shanice said.

Looking Curtis in the eye, Renee leaned back and took a slow sip of water. The young man blushed. Satisfied that at least one person in her vicinity had the decency to want her, she was ready to order. "I'll have the same."

Curtis curtsied before going back into the kitchen.

Once alone, Shanice leaned in. "Why didn't you tell me about Dorothy?"

"If Barbara didn't tell you, it wasn't my place to bring it up. How did you find out?"

"Lisa told me, unintentionally."

"You found her? Good. She's the one the police should be harassing, not me." Renee pouted.

"I'll get to that later. Tell me about Ms. Barbara and Pastor Robinson."

Renee cast a glance around the nearly empty restaurant. The customers closest to them were five booths away and that couple was engrossed in their own drama. She pulled a salt and pepper shaker to the center of the table. "A long time ago, two friends become lovers. They got married and, over time, realized it was a mistake. Unfortunately, a public break in their personal relationship would jeopardize the organization they had created." She put the sugar dispenser next to the salt. "Rather than divorce, they agreed to quietly pursue outside arrangements."

Shanice pushed the seasonings to the side. "Lisa suggested that Ms. Barbara had stopped being satisfied with that arrangement."

"Over time, she felt like she was living a lie and divorce is no longer a badge of shame. Walter was still against any legal dissolution, though. It's strange to talk about this in the past tense." Renee stared down at her mat. "Where did you find Lisa?"

"Can't tell you that. She changed her number because she'd been getting harassing phone calls. She doesn't know anything about the pictures."

Renee sucked her teeth. "Maybe that's why she was so fidgety during our sessions. She's too fragile to perform in front of critics if she falls apart over a crank call."

"The messages rattled her."

"I block calls and move on. You can't let random weirdos get into your head like that."

"And you have a lot of experience with this?"

"My business number is on the website. Anyone can call it now."

Curtis returned with lunch. The thick sandwiches were buried under mounds of dill-flavored potato chips. After washing down a few bites, Shanice eased back into conversation. "Why happened with Detective Gerard?"

"Monday, not long after you left, he came to the studio for a chat. He was official but friendly. This morning, he threatened to arrest me." Renee dabbed at the crumbs in the corner of her mouth. "He played that damned message I left for Barbara and started shouting questions at me. 'Weren't you jealous of Mrs. Robinson?' 'Do you think she got what she deserved?' Then, that man stood in my living room and accused me of being Walter's girlfriend." The idea physically repulsed her.

It was the perfect opening for the subject Shanice wanted to tactfully bring up. "Nothing to worry about if you have an alibi."

"I was at Sparrow Baptist trying to teach their young adult choir a new song. Gerard claims I could have slipped out, ran the five blocks to New Hope, killed Barbara, and run back – all while wearing lavender stilettos."

"He's just fishing," Shanice said. "Gerard accused me of sleeping with Pastor Robinson too. He likes to rattle people."

"Walter had no business getting me involved in this. If that detective comes back, I'm going to tell him about the pictures."

Shanice imagined her ex thoughtlessly putting everyone in jeopardy. "Sure. Do that. Wag your tongue and cut your own throat. You'd have to explain why your protégée is in them and why the pastor hired your ex-lover to act as a go-between."

Renee's smirk disappeared as she thought through the consequences of the threat. She sighed. "I'm just saying that a man in his position should be careful about accusing others."

"You think he killed Ms. Barbara?" Shanice suddenly felt queasy.

"No, but I wouldn't be surprised if Oliver had something to do with it."

"Oliver? The organist? Why would he be involved?"

The smirk returned. Renee took a teasing bite of pickle. "You didn't know Walter has a boyfriend?"

And Shanice shut right up.

Chapter 19

Debra stood in front of the prepared foods section of The Chopin Cart, unsure of what to do. A home-cooked meal was the perfect opportunity to impress; the usual taco kit wouldn't do. On the other hand, her employee discount wouldn't do much to defray the cost of the higher end meals.

Thinking back to their conversation, Cynthia hadn't mentioned any dietary restrictions. She had, however, offered to bring dessert. "Do you like it savory or sweet?"

Debra tried to sound nonchalant. "Whatever you bring will be fine. I can take it however you dish it out."

The velvet laugh on the other end of the line scattered the butterflies in her stomach. "Don't be so sure about that. I'm known for testing culinary limits."

"I look forward to the challenge."

And it would be a challenge to get dressed, heat up dinner, and clean up before company arrived. Debra refocused on the task at hand. After wavering between a heat-and-serve rack of lamb and a Meatloaf-in-Minutes, she settled for honey-glazed pork roast, garlic string beans sautéed with almonds, and basmati rice.

As soon as she got home, Debra turned on the oven and headed for the shower. After transforming day-old rotisserie chicken into chicken salad, she smelled like ranch dressing. The stress and frustration of the day melted away when the hot water hit her skin.

Towel draped around her, Debra peeked into the bedroom next to hers. "Hey, what's up? You ready for dinner?"

Shanice lay on the bed clutching a balled-up piece of paper, a bag of cheese curls at her side. "Don't know if I'd be good company tonight. I'm not feeling sociable."

"You have to come down. I can't leave Cynthia alone with Gina. Plus, you'll feel better after you have a decent meal."

"Slapping an 'organic' sticker on a Box O' Taco doesn't make it healthy."

"We're having roast pork with vegetables."

Shanice perked up. "Okay, I'm in."

"Great! Go downstairs and put it in the oven for me."

Debra confronted the next obstacle – her closet. She decided on a fitted burgundy shirt and black slacks. She could have gotten away with jeans and a T-shirt, but that was what she was wearing when they met.

She considered cologne, but the scent from her peppermint body butter hadn't quite dissipated yet. *Besides, who casually lounges around the house in a cloud of scent? I'm overthinking this; it's only dinner.* She slid on her faux leather clogs and went downstairs.

Shanice had cleared away the books and junk mail that usually cluttered the dining room table. Now she arranged place settings. "A meal of this caliber deserves cloth napkins."

"This is great! The food is on?"

"Gina is handling that."

That news calmed Debra's anxiety. "When did she come in?"

Shanice shrugged. "She and Childress were working in the basement when I got back."

Gina was on tiptoe reaching for a serving dish when Debra went into the kitchen. "Wait, let me get that for you."

"It's about time you showed up." Gina tucked a loose piece of hair back under her headscarf and readjusted the apron covering her overalls. "Why are we preparing for your date?"

Debra blushed. "It's not a date. Cynthia is coming over to apologize to you."

"Whatever." Gina rolled her eyes but couldn't stop herself from smiling. "All of the food should be ready in about twenty minutes. You better fix her plate. I don't want that woman searching my cupboards."

Debra threw away the containers and wrappers emblazoned with the Chopin Cart logo. "There's one small thing – I gave Cynthia the impression that I'd be cooking dinner from scratch."

"Your secret is safe with me."

"Thank you!" Debra gave Gina a hug.

"Get off. Let me get ready, before your girl confuses me with a maid."

When the bell rang, Debra waited a full fifteen seconds before opening the door to the radiant smile of her guest. "Hi."

Cynthia wrapped a stiff arm around her shoulder. "Hey, sweetie! How are you?" She held up a lemon pound cake from a cheap supermarket chain. "My pantry was a little sparse, but I hope this will do."

Shanice stepped forward and took the dessert. "Hi, I'm Shanice. Nice to meet you. I'll put this away until later." After a quick handshake, she disappeared into the kitchen.

Debra led Cynthia to the sofa and, after making sure she was comfortable, produced the tiny gold butterfly that prompted the visit. "This belongs to you."

Cynthia took the post off the earring and put it back in her ear. "Of course! This is my favorite, so it's always falling out. Thank you."

"How was your day?" Debra asked.

"Okay."

"What did you do? Anything exciting?"

Gina came down the stairs with her head wrapped in a new scarf and a clean but worn sweat suit. "Excuse my appearance, but after dinner, I'm going to get back to work."

"She's restoring parts of the basement," Debra

explained.

Rising with the grace of a dancer, Cynthia rushed over to Gina. "I'm so sorry about yesterday. I was trying to pay you a compliment, and between my brain and my mouth, it got all twisted up and backwards."

Gina put a reassuring hand on her shoulder. "No worries. It was the end of a challenging day and I was tired." She glanced over at the coffee table. "No one has offered you a drink?"

Debra rolled her eyes. "I haven't gotten around to that yet."

"No, you relax. You deserve a break after all that cooking you've done." Gina turned back to Cynthia. "Is red wine okay?"

"That would be great." When she walked away, Cynthia returned to the sofa and slid closer to Debra. "Are those two together?" she asked, pointing towards the kitchen.

"No, just friends." Then Debra added quickly, "All of us have only been friends. No exes or weird relationship dynamics here."

Cynthia took out her phone and shrank back into her corner.

Gina and Shanice returned with laughter, wine glasses, and a bottle of merlot. Gina distributed coasters. "Guess who almost put her eye out pulling out the cork?"

Shanice gave her a dirty look before filling the glasses. "It tried to attack me, but I was brave."

Debra checked her watch. She was ready for the evening to be over. "Did either of you check the oven?"

"The roast is resting and the rolls are browning," Gina said. "We'll be eating very soon." After a few seconds passed awkwardly, she took a sip and smiled at Cynthia. "Debra explained your dissertation. How is it coming along?"

"Slow. People have no problem sharing their stories, but they don't answer questions. On the other hand, it's given me the chance to scout out apartments in the area."

Debra seized the opening. "You're thinking about

coming to Maynard? Where are you living now?"

Cynthia frowned. "I'm staying with an aunt in Griffin Hill. The neighborhood has a reputation, but I never felt unsafe. Then someone walked into the church around the corner and beat a woman to death. A friend on the force actually thought he was consoling me by revealing it wasn't a random crime."

The housemates shifted uncomfortably, a cloud of gloom settling all around them. "Everyone was shocked to hear about Ms. Barbara," Gina said. "I grew up in Hope Reborn."

"The music drew me in once or twice, but I never got around to joining the church." Cynthia turned to Shanice, who was staring into her glass. "Aren't you a member?"

"No," Shanice responded without looking up. "I don't go there."

"But, Shanice, I'm sure I've seen you there."

Debra ears began itching. "What are you really doing here?"

Cynthia's face curdled like sour cream. "What do you mean? I left my earring –"

"Yeah, you left it; you didn't lose it. What are you really doing here?"

Leaning forward, Cynthia met their challenging glares with her own. "I am a journalist, working on a series about crooked ministers. A lot of these storefront con men have criminal records or hop from church to church to outrun a scandal. I put my last story on hold when this thing with Barbara Robinson happened."

"It's not a thing that happened," Shanice said. "She was murdered."

"Yeah, and I know there's more to it than a homeless man gone psycho. You were there. What did you see? More importantly, what is your connection with Pastor Robinson?"

Gina was at the end of her hospitality. "How did you get her name? How did you know to come to this house?"

"Don't you listen?" Cynthia rolled her eyes. "I have a friend on the force. I've read the police report."

Shanice stood up. "I have nothing to say to you."

"Robinson, a known womanizer, is found standing over his wife's corpse with a woman who's not a member of his church. Who is this Shanice Wilkins? Why does this mystery woman remain in the shadows? Is she a mistress? A love child?" Cynthia softened her voice, her lips curved into a condescending smile. "If you won't tell me the story, I'll have to fill the gaps with my own imagination."

Debra grabbed her guest by the elbow. "It's time for you to go."

Cynthia pulled away. "How would the owner of the Chopin Cart or the CEO of the Waybert-Slone Foundation feel about having an employee involved with a high-profile murder?"

"What's the problem here, ladies?" Everyone turned around to see Childress. Out of uniform and covered in sweat, the authoritative edge in her voice trumped her appearance.

Shanice was grateful for the intrusion. "Officer Childress, this reporter is threatening to spread lies about us if I don't give her an interview."

"I remember you." The policewoman laughed. "Craig brought you to Captain Burke's retirement party. He enjoyed showing you off." She closed her eyes and sorted through her mental filing cabinet. "Ceeda Truth, gossip blogger turned reporter for the *Edmondson Enquirer*."

Cynthia's bravado evaporated. "The public has a right to know the truth," she sputtered.

Childress sighed heavily. "Gerard's going to flip when he finds out Craig can't keep his mouth shut when his fly is open. As for you, judges frown on people who try to intimidate witnesses. I'm sure your employer doesn't approve of that method either."

Cynthia gathered up her purse and stood. "No, this has all been a big misunderstanding."

"That's good to hear," said Childress as she walked the reporter to the door. "One libelous word from you about any of these ladies and you'll be the news story."

For the second time that week, Cynthia made a quick escape.

Gina raised her glass to Childress. "Our knight in grimy armor."

Childress tipped an imaginary cap. "I heard loud voices and decided to investigate."

"Shanice, I'm so sorry," Debra said. "The post was on the earring when I found it, so I knew she was lying about it falling out. I thought it was an excuse to see me again."

"It's all right," Shanice said, finally loosening her grip on the glass.

"I feel so stupid." Debra put her head in her hands.

"It's not your fault," Childress said. "Cynthia befriends people to manipulate them into doing what she wants."

Gina stretched. "She better not bring those ashy legs across my threshold again." She looked at Childress. "I can't let you walk out of here empty-handed. Nope, no argument, you're joining us for dinner. I'll set the food out." She took the bottle of wine with her.

"Could Cynthia really make more trouble for us?" Shanice asked.

"It's unlikely," Childress said. "She's jeopardized her source within the department, so she'll probably lay low for a while. I can't promise other reporters won't try to contact you, but there have been three more homicides since Ms. Barbara was killed."

"Was her source correct about the murder not being random?"

"It's too early for absolutes; the investigation is ongoing. A guy showed up at a soup kitchen not far from Hope Reborn wearing a scarf that had an excess of dried blood on it. He had open warrants for breaking and entering, so he's been taken into custody. After the scarf and other clothing items are tested, we may be adding a murder charge."

Debra sat up. "He's the killer?"

"If he's not, we'll keep plugging away until we catch the bad guy." Childress noticed Shanice staring at the ground. "Is it just the reporter bothering you? There's not something else I should know, is there?"

"Unfortunately, yes," Gina said. She walked toward them with the cake. "Dessert expired three days ago."

After seeing Childress out and clearing the dishes away, the trio settled back around the dining room table and Shanice relayed the story about finding Lisa. She kept the new revelations about the Robinsons to herself.

 Debra took out her notebook and pen. "And you're convinced Lisa is telling the truth?"

Shanice frowned. "She has no idea what's happening, and I've given her something else to worry about."

"What's our next step?" Debra asked.

Gina exhaled loudly. "Next step? Are you kidding? When it was a chat with the ex, that was fine. Threatening phones calls, harassment, and murder – stop pretending that this isn't dangerous? What if the person at the other end of the lens is the killer?"

Debra rolled her eyes. "The goal of blackmail is to make money and you can't do that if the victim is dead. The murder has probably shaken him up. By now, he's probably deleted the pictures and hopes no one comes looking for him as a suspect."

"That's an even better reason to let this go," Gina said. "Why stir up trouble?"

Shanice touched Gina's arm. "Finding a person is not the same as confronting them. I admit, I was reckless in dealing with Lisa because I didn't think of her as a threat. I wouldn't do that again." Then she turned to Debra. "There is no next step. Tomorrow, I'm telling Pastor Robinson the trail has gone cold. "

Debra tapped her pen against the table. "That's because you jumped into the middle of the mess instead of starting at the beginning. How it was done will lead us to who done it."

"Us?" Gina and Shanice said in unison.

"Yes, us." A sly smile spread across Debra's lips. "I have a plan."

Chapter 20

Sitting in the Montgomery Cove parking lot the next morning, Shanice took the crumpled paper from her pocket and smoothed it out against the steering wheel. The thick black block letters pasted on the page issued a warning: Mind Your Business Or You'll End Up Like Barbara.

Lisa's story about finding a note on her car reminded Shanice of the flier waiting on the windshield when she left New Life Sanctuary. She rediscovered it after driving Renee home from lunch. This threat and the drama of Debra's new friend had made for a sleepless night.

How many people knew why the Robinsons really hired her? Was Gina right about the blackmailer also being the killer? Someone was obviously following her; had she put Lisa in danger?

Shanice was scared but angry. If someone was stalking her, she wanted to stare that person in the face. She didn't want to be like Lisa, jumping every time she met a new person.

She didn't want her housemates involved. If there was legal trouble down the road, she hoped their ignorance would keep them safe. That was why she initially discouraged the plan. Still, the idea seemed harmless enough and Gina would be there to keep Debra out of trouble.

While they were away, Shanice could work unfettered. She stuffed the paper back into her pocket and sent a text to Pastor Robinson announcing her unexpected arrival. She was eager to see his reaction to the message.

The Bitmore-Key Inn gave out-of-town guests the impression that it was a full-service resort. The photo gallery on its website featured image after image of rolling green hills, tennis courts, and golf courses. These things were part of the magnificent views from the rooms at the top level – the sixth floor. When guests tried to access the promised land from the ground floor, they found the cobblestone path led to and traveled alongside a decorative hedge border. The property they were gazing at from above actually belonged to the gated community next door.

The BKI was impressive in its own way. The gravel driveway leading up to the entrance did wind its way uphill through seasonal gardens and past a fountain depicting the muses. Shielded by trees at the front, it was easy to imagine that one was at a country retreat far away from the garish lights and havoc of the city. "Come," the stone façade archway over the entrance seemed to say, "leave your troubles and burdens behind and reunite with nature." It was the perfect quiet retreat for writers or a distraction-free corporate meeting.

When the doorman opened the door to her cab and offered a gloved hand to help her to her feet, Gina was almost under the Bitmore-Key spell. Her lungs filled with fresh air, and for a moment, she forgot that downtown Ardola was less than twenty minutes away. Then she walked into the lobby and the art-deco-inspired furniture destroyed the country cottage feel.

"Good morning," the clerk at the registration desk announced with a smile that showcased his perfectly bonded teeth. "How can I help you?" The name "Rob" gleamed on his nametag.

"Gina Smallwood, I have a reservation. Early check-in."

Unseen fingers tapped away furiously. "You'll only be staying for one night?" He peeked over the counter and the smile dimmed when he noticed her lack of luggage.

"The house is being repainted and I need a break from the fumes." She patted her over-sized shoulder bag.

"Everything I need is right here."

"I understand." Rob programmed an electronic key. "You'll only need one?" When she nodded, he put the plastic card and a brochure in an envelope. "You'll be in room 652, which has a great, relaxing view of the golf course and lake. For added relaxation, I've also included information about L'Aurore, our award-winning European spa."

"As opposed to the Ethiopian one?"

"Excuse me?"

"Never mind."

The walk to the elevator bank took her past several brightly lit boutique shops. Gina didn't find expensive scarves draped over curve-less mannequins and cruise-ship quality jewelry enticing, but she did plan to have a drink or two by the reflecting pool.

Room 652 had a queen-sized bed, nightstands, a glass-topped desk, and a flat-screen TV on a wooden dresser. Over the bed was a photo of plump fruit spilling out of an ornate bowl. The room appeared designed to make people want to spend as little time as possible inside.

Gina was happy to oblige. This was her part in Debra's scheme, to lounge around and take note of anyone acting suspicious. It was silly but spending a night away from home and putting some temporal space between her and that Cynthia madness would be good.

After putting her clothes and toiletries away, Gina touched up her brows. It was time for a late breakfast.

Debra didn't have to go in to work until the afternoon; she celebrated by spending an extra fifteen minutes under the covers. Her stomach churned. Giving up on rest, she sat on the side of the bed and sulked.

Shanice and Gina said it wasn't her fault, but there was no one else to take the blame. She had invited a stranger into their home – twice – and endangered her friends. If she had met Cynthia online or at the club, their first few hangout sessions would have been limited to meeting for coffee or the movies.

When Cynthia revealed her true intentions, she had sat on the sofa, stunned into silence. If Childress hadn't been there to save the day...

Debra looked up Cynthia's alter ego "Ceeda Truth" and found a barrage of inflammatory columns that were equal parts gossip and fact. *Which city councilmen owe back child support? Which pastor has left a trail of Ponzi schemes behind him? Which minister got his wrists broken when he laid hands on the gangbanger's girlfriend?* This was what she had invited inside, all because of a brief encounter on the sidewalk.

Maybe last night's fiasco inadvertently saved them in the long run. Dating Cynthia would have been disastrous. With a little skill and more patience, what secrets could the reporter have teased out into the open? How many coy smiles and nuzzles before she started talking about Shanice, the church, and the pictures?

Debra bristled. *Those damn pictures.*

Venturing out of her room, she listened at the top of the steps and was greeted with silence. She was happy to be alone. By the time they met tonight – if everyone had played their part – Cynthia would be a distant memory.

Debra believed the aspiring blackmailer had to be an employee at the Bitmore-Key Inn. Experience taught her that customers don't censor conversations in front of uniformed service workers. In the Chopin Cart break room, her coworkers traded stories about patrons planning rendezvous with each other's spouses or strategizing ways to hide money from a soon-to-be ex.

If people let these things casually slip out while waiting in line for cold cuts, what did hotel employees overhear? A bartender, a housekeeper, or a front desk attendant could have easily seen or heard something unbecoming of a minister's wife and decided to take a few quick photos. Who else could easily acquire a card key for the hotel room?

The beauty of the plan was that there was no need to

find and accuse an actual person. If they successfully tested the theory tonight, Shanice could present it to her client and the case would be solved.

The minister would get peace of mind and Shanice could stay clear of the police.

In the meantime, Debra slipped on her robe and got back to work on writing *Fresh Cuts,* her horror novel set in a grocery store. She decided to add a new character to the chaos – a gossip columnist who tried to escape the plague by hiding in the walk-in freezer only to become lunch for the zombie chickens gathered there.

Chapter 21

Shanice readied her photo ID for the guard, but he waved her through. "Pastor Robinson called down and said to let you up. Damn shame what happened to Mrs. Robinson. She was a genuinely good person. When my wife got sick and I needed time off to take care of her, she made sure I had a job to come back to."

He pointed to a pot of lilies that took up a third of the desk. "Can you take this up to him? People keep dropping stuff off here when it should be sent to the funeral home. Tenants complain if this area starts to look cluttered; when I refuse delivery, they complain that I'm heartless."

Shanice picked up the vase. "There's no pleasing some people."

The woman who answered the Robinson's door was a slightly younger version of Barbara. She wore fitted blue jeans and had a silver cross sitting on her white blouse. Her hair was curled into a tight mushroom bob that barely moved as she stationed herself in the doorframe and raised her incredibly arched eyebrows. "Can I help you?"

"I'm Shanice Wilkins. Pastor Robinson is expecting me."

"Ann-Louise, let the young lady in. I told you I had to tend to some church business this morning."

She moved back reluctantly. "Can't be too careful. The security in this building leaves something to be desired."

Sitting in the dining room, Pastor Robinson looked as if he were withering away inside his burgundy tracksuit. In front of him sat a barely disturbed plate of eggs, sausage, and toast. "Ms. Wilkins is our web designer. The website was one of the last projects Barbara undertook and I want it to continue. Ms. Wilkins, this is Barbara's sister, Ann-Louise."

Shanice set the vase on a table next to another cluster of flowers and extended a hand. "I'm sorry about Ms. Barbara. I only met her recently, but I know she was a lovely person."

Ann-Louise's face eased into a sad smile "Thank you for your words of comfort. Some people nearly knock me over to give Walter a shoulder to cry on. She's not even in the ground yet and some vulture came through here ready to claim her wardrobe for the clothing ministry."

Pastor Robinson tried to be diplomatic. "People grieve in their own way. They're trying to be helpful."

"They should know real family trumps church family." She turned to Shanice. "You know what would be nice? A memorial on the computer. Can you do that? Are you going to film the funeral and put it on the cable access channel?"

That caught Shanice off guard. "I could include a page on the site dedicated to her memory –"

"Ann-Louise, please." The minister's voice was tired. "I can't let you get involved in official church business."

"No worries. I'm off to the grocery store. It used to be that people would bring real food when they came to sit with the family. Today, people stop off on the way and get a bucket of chicken. It's not healthy at all." She beckoned Shanice closer and whispered, "Come lock up behind me."

At the door, Ann-Louise teared up. "I know who you are. You were with Walter in that Sunday school room. Thank you. When a person dies a violent death, sometimes it takes a moment for them to understand that they are dead. I'm glad that there were people who cared about her there, that love was in the room when she passed over. I'm so thankful that hate wasn't what she left here with." She squeezed Shanice's arm before leaving.

Pastor Robinson invited her into his office. Immediately, her attention was drawn to a painting on the wall opposite the desk. Full of vibrant hues, it depicted the sun rising over a seaside town. Golden rays of orange and yellow spread along the blue water and reflected from shop windows. Figures lay on the beach and strolled down a cobblestone lane; there was no urgency. Shanice could easily imagine the minister using it for meditation.

Unlike the church office, there was no chair for a guest. Shanice felt awkward standing there. "Your sister-in-law seems nice."

"Ann-Louise is a blessing and a curse. She's been dealing with the funeral home, keeping pressure on the police, and making sure the church doesn't overwhelm me. With everyone underfoot, there's not time to just be. I miss Barbara so much."

When he covered his eyes with a handkerchief, Shanice looked away. Unsure of what to say, she concentrated on a shelf displaying an array of religious figurines. After a moment, the sobs subsided. "Do you have any news?" he asked.

"I found Lisa."

Life sprang back into his eyes. "Who is she? Why did she do this to us?"

"She didn't. Lisa has a sensitive job that would be put in jeopardy if she was ever outed. Like Renee, she's somewhat paranoid about people finding out. She confirmed that nothing scandalous happened that weekend or any weekend. She had no idea pictures existed."

"I don't believe it."

Shanice tried to keep her voice even. "I do. She told me more of the truth than you or Ms. Barbara did. Why didn't you tell me about Dorothy?"

Pastor Robinson grabbed the edge of the desk as if to steady himself. "Barbara and Dorothy's friendship has nothing to do with this. More importantly, it's none of your business."

"It's my business when you invited me into the situation."

"No, Ms. Wilkins. You are confused." He enveloped her in a cold, icy stare. "Barbara did not have a romantic relationship with Lisa. That is the lie and the only thing you need to be concerned about. Any trickery or deception you feel comes from your own misguided assumptions."

Shanice was speechless. She didn't know what to expect when she laid the truth in front of him, but it wasn't this. The Robinsons had been married for decades; this wouldn't have been the first time he had to deal with someone who stumbled across their secret. The skillful orator knew how to manipulate emotions, but he had a point.

Pastor Robinson cleared his throat. "Lisa has to be involved. Unless you know who took the pictures inside the hotel room?"

"Maybe it was the person who left this on my windshield." Shanice handed him the note and watched carefully as he unfolded it.

His hands trembled. "I don't understand."

"Lisa's been receiving her own threats. That's why she changed her number. Who else knows that you asked me to look into this? It has to be someone in your circle of friends."

Pastor Robinson looked sick. "I can't imagine any of our close friends would betray us."

Though tempted, Shanice felt it was a bad time to remind him that Renee once had been considered a friend. Having the upper hand didn't feel good. Watching fear settle onto his already weary shoulders, she pitied him. "How about this? Why don't we check the postmark on the envelope against your address book and see if any zip codes match? The person who did this probably wasn't sophisticated enough to mail this too far from home."

"There's no postmark on the original envelope."

"I thought you got it through the mail?"

Pastor Robinson unlocked a desk drawer, withdrew the envelope with the remaining pictures, and handed it to her. It was a plain brown envelope with his name written on it.

"No stamp, postmark, or return address. Thursday afternoon, it was just sitting on my desk."

"At church?" Shanice couldn't believe it. All this time, she assumed the photographs had been mailed to the condo. "Doesn't Sarah open all of your mail? She had to see the envelope – if she didn't put it on the desk herself."

"It can't be her. Sarah doesn't come in at all Wednesday or Thursday."

"Who would have access to the church after hours?"

"People are in and out of church all day. The janitor leaves the side door open half of the time."

"Are you sure that over the years, someone at church hasn't figured out that your marriage wasn't typical? If I could find out –"

The minister pivoted toward the window. "Impossible. It would be part of the other gossip whispered through the congregation. We would know if anyone suspected."

Shanice's mind was racing. The person tormenting the Robinsons came from their own circle, maybe their own congregation, and Pastor Robinson knew it. He had to know. The blame-Renee-find-Lisa business was an exercise in denial.

Without warning, he snatched up the envelope and the threat. By the time Shanice realized he was feeding the documents into a paper shredder hidden behind his desk, it was too late to save them. "What are you doing? That's evidence. The police could have gotten fingerprints off that or something."

"It doesn't matter now. Barbara's gone and some doors don't need to be opened."

Suddenly, voices drifted in from the living room and Shanice swallowed her other questions. Ann-Louise had returned – not with food, but with women of varying ages. Wearing loose house dresses and protective scarfs, they carried brooms, mops, and buckets. Shanice recognized Deaconess Cheryl from the church office.

"I'm sorry, Walter," Anne Louise said, ushering the

group inside. "I forgot that the deaconesses were coming over to help clean up."

There was a flash of exasperation in Pastor Robinson's eyes. He met the new visitors with a weary smile. Eying her suspiciously, the ladies murmured a greeting at Shanice before inundating the pastor with hugs. "Ladies, I'm sorry. I'll have to excuse myself. Sleep has been eluding me, so I have to catch a nap when the moment strikes." He turned to Shanice. "Let's stick with doing the tribute page. You can get archival material from Bruce Pruitt on the audio/video team. Maybe you can interview members of the congregation, too? Give them the chance to share personal stories about Barbara."

As he retreated, the group migrated to Shanice like pigeons fighting over bread crumbs.

Ann-Louise beamed with pride. "You know, the memorial was my idea."

Chapter 22

As the elevator began to descend, Shanice made a snap decision not to return to the lobby. Oliver Davis, church organist and lover of Pastor Robinson, lived on the fourth floor. According to Renee, the men had been together for over a decade. Shanice had to speak to him. Someone had threatened her life and she wanted to know who.

Shanice got off on the fourth floor and slowly walked down the corridor while tapping away at her phone. The white doors with glowing red doorbells all looked the same. Doing a quick online search for Oliver's address didn't help.

It was time to take a risk. Shanice rang the doorbell for 4E and pretended to be confused when a white woman holding a toddler answered the door. "Hi," she began clearly uneasy. "Is Mr. Davis here?"

"Nope," the woman said as the baby pulled at her earrings. "This is the Finley's. Who are you looking for?"

"Oliver Davis, the organist of Hope Reborn Baptist church."

"I don't know his name, but," the woman leaned over to whisper, "the black guy in 4G is a musician."

"Thank you."

Once in front of 4G, Shanice heard soft piano chords. The lanky man who answered the door wore a royal blue robe over blue pinstriped pajamas. His facial features were soft, but his eyes were like cold steel. "Can I help you?"

Shanice bent the truth. "Mr. Oliver Davis? I'm Shanice Wilkins, the church webmaster. Pastor Robinson said I should talk to you about contributing to a memorial page for his late wife."

Oliver sneered, "You must be the dyke detective. Come on in."

She followed him into a room that looked like it spilled from the pages of a luxury catalog. It was the same floor plan as the Robinsons' unit, but the flowing tapestries made it look bigger. Prominent in the living room was a painting that resembled the piece in Pastor Robinson's office, though it was set at dusk.

Oliver pointed at a pitcher filled with an amber liquid on a rolling cart. "Sweet tea?" Shanice nodded and he poured out a glass for her. As she accepted it, she noticed his lean but muscular fingers. "Walter would have called first if he sent you, so no more tales. What are you doing here?"

Shanice settled on the corner of a chaise lounge. "Pastor has at least ten people with him. I have some questions that need answers and I know you two are very close."

Oliver took a slow sip from his glass before sitting at his piano stool. "What exactly is it that you think you know?" His tone had changed slightly to a defensive one.

If she said the wrong thing, she'd be on the other side of the door before getting to the bottom of the glass. "That the Robinsons were married in the legal sense only. Ms. Barbara had Dorothy; Pastor Robinson has you."

"Renee told you?" Cursing under his breath, Oliver lifted his eyes to the ceiling. "For a woman with a secret, she sure can't keep one. Hard to believe she's not the linchpin in all this."

"Her point was that other people may have reasons to blackmail the Robinsons. The way the pictures were left on Pastor Robinson's desk suggests someone familiar with daily activity at church." Shanice waited for a reaction. There was none, so she pushed further. "Since they happened within days of each other, I'm wondering if the photographs and the murder are connected."

Oliver gave her a sidelong glance. "You can't lay this at the feet of our congregation. There's plenty of petty jealousies and backbiting in Hope Reborn but nothing escalating to murder. Why kill someone in cold blood when you can spread malicious gossip and assassinate them every Sunday?"

"It wasn't cold-blooded. This was explosive, angry – someone who hadn't intended to kill."

"Like a homeless man who thought he could snatch a purse without the victim putting up a fight?" His tense frown turned into a condescending smile. "You're biting off a little more than you can chew. It's not official, but the police have already arrested someone. I'm happy to trust they know what they're doing."

Shanice shrugged. "Do a lot of people have keys to the church? Do you?"

"Of course. I'm the Minister of Music. The availability of the sanctuary for choir rehearsal will not be at the whim of a tipsy janitor."

"And you have keys to Pastor Robinson's office?"

Oliver's eyes danced in amusement. "What are you trying to ask me?"

No one knows where I am, Shanice thought. She was in a stranger's apartment, about to delicately suggest he had a motive for blackmail, perhaps even murder. It was dangerous and foolish, but she might not have a chance to speak to Oliver again.

"I know it's hard to love someone and have your world confined to a few square feet," she began. "Dating Renee was nearly impossible. It didn't take long before I got tired of being her secret. How has it been for you? I've seen the Sunday service. Pastor Robinson grabs and hugs other men in greeting as they walk around for the offering. You're steps away from him for the whole service and he barely glances your way. You must have envied the woman he shared his public life with, even if it was all for show."

Oliver turned to the keyboard and began playing softly. "Barbara, Walter, and I have a history. Long ago, before your parents probably met, the three of us were in seminary.

Barbara and I became fast friends; we picked up on each other as family. Then Walter came into the picture. He and I started a casual relationship.

"Next thing I knew, they were engaged. She convinced him that the Lord drew them together because they could understand the other's struggle with unnatural urges. They got married to heal each other. I was exiled." Oliver looked over his shoulder at Shanice. "If there was ever a time I could have killed Barbara, it was then. She knew I was in love with Walter but too afraid to tell him."

Though she felt sympathy for him, Shanice stayed focused. "You've been dating him in secret all this time?"

Oliver's laugh reverberated off the walls. "No, sweetie. They came down here to start Hope Reborn. I decided it was New York, not God, that was calling me." He pointed at a bookshelf. "Second row, third book from the left – take a look at that."

The heavy photo album featured a guitarist with a bright red Jheri curl and skintight pants. "Wow," Shanice said. "This is you?"

"In the eighties, I wore mascara, high heel boots, and my curls laid better than any wig. I did a lot of studio work, toured with a couple of bands, spent many a night behind a fog machine. Four years later, Walter was in my apartment admitting he had made a mistake and could we pick up where we had left off. He even had a letter from Barbara apologizing."

"That's when you got back together?"

"No, I was having too much fun. I wasn't interested in love anymore."

Shanice closed the book. "Eventually, you forgave him."

Oliver stopped playing. "AIDS showed up and the party was over. Seeing friends and lovers fade away to dust, it does something to you. I needed to get away from death. I moved up to Albany and started playing organ for a little church there. A loveless life is its own kind of death. Eventually, Walter convinced me to come back to him."

"No hard feelings with Barbara?"

"None at all. She became my sister."

Shanice suddenly felt guilty. She was so concerned about questioning Oliver that she didn't think to offer him comfort or compassion. "I'm sorry." It sounded hollow.

He acknowledged her belated condolences with a slight nod and continued. "We purposely created our public personas. Walter, the man of God who is weak in matters of the female flesh. Barbara, the righteous wife who kept him from straying too far. Oliver, Barbara's best friend that Walter could barely tolerate. Don't you understand? We gave each other cover. When Barbara left to take care of Dorothy, everyone knew Walter behaved himself because I was her eyes and ears."

His eyes blurred with tears. "Barbara's not even in the ground yet and some women have already put their bid in to be the next Mrs. Robinson. It's disgusting. They'll only allow Walter to be a grieving widower for so long. I don't know what we're going to do."

Shanice thanked him for his candor and left. She thought Oliver's fear had him imagining problems that did not exist. *Who would question the orientation of an elderly widower devoted to the memory of his late wife?*

As Shanice walked by the security desk, she noted an older black woman standing to the side with a covered dish. The lady took out a small compact to check there was no lipstick on her teeth and giggled nervously before walking toward the elevator.

In the parking lot, Shanice found Detective Gerard leaning against the trunk of her car. "Spare a few moments, Ms. Wilkins?"

"Do I have a choice?"

"You do." He scratched at the scraggly beard on his chin. "I need your help."

Shanice folded her arms. "I'm listening."

"Ms. Barbara's sister told me that you will be interviewing attendees of the funeral. I'd like you to keep your eyes and ears open; make note of anyone acting strange."

"Anyone? Does this mean you've stopped looking for Pastor Robinson's imaginary girlfriend?"

He laughed. "That's only one of several theories we're exploring. You're the webmaster, right? One of the in crowd. Church folks might talk a little freer around you."

Shanice sidestepped around him to the door. "I don't think I can help you. I wouldn't know what to look for."

"It's easy, Ms. Wilkins." Detective Gerard straightened up. "If you come across someone who makes you more nervous than I do, that's the person I need to talk to." He chuckled before nodding and walking away.

Chapter 23

Arriving a few minutes early for a seven o'clock dinner reservation, Gina couldn't resist the bowl of nuts at the bar. Helena, a masseuse at L'Aurore, had squeezed a week's worth of stress out of her muscles but left her famished. The berry-infused water the spa served as a treat afterward only aggravated her hunger.

She eased into the worn leather seat and ordered fruit punch with a touch of Grand Marnier. The bar was bathed in a warm amber glow. At the other end of the lounge, a host wearing a tuxedo stood at a podium to welcome diners into La Petite Grange, the main restaurant.

Whatever sophistication the lounge tried to evoke was overshadowed by its patrons. The Bitmore-Key was the overflow hotel for a national carpentry convention. The jazz trio playing in the corner was drowned out by alcohol-tinged laughter and spirited discussions about wood.

First came the scent – a striking mix of clove and cinnamon, then came the man. He was in his early fifties and, though all his hair was black, the hairpiece was a distinctly different texture. He had narrow shoulders and a broad paunch sitting snugly on top of his belt.

"A filly like you is too lovely to spend this beautiful evening alone." He ran his tongue over bonded teeth before extending his hand. "I'm Billy. My associates and I would love for you to join us at our table." He motioned behind him to a group of similar-looking fellows with wrinkles that looked older than her.

"Thank you, but I'm waiting for a friend."

"Can't be a man," Billy roared. "No fellow worth his salt would make you wait."

This made Gina laugh. "You're right."

"Well, I've done my job by getting you to smile. If your friend doesn't show, come on over. Promise we won't bore you with tales of the trade." Billy did a little bow, his hairpiece threatening to tip over, before returning to his group.

Gina turned to find Shanice at her elbow. "What did I miss?"

"Not much. A group of cabinetmakers tried to seduce me."

Shanice looked suspiciously at Gina's glass. "Somebody buy you a drink?"

"Drink? I was this close to getting a free dinner." Twisting in her seat, Gina realized Shanice was alone. "Where's Debra?"

"She called me earlier; there's some type of emergency at the store. We should start dinner without her."

Gina's fingertips felt the bottom of the bowl and came to a sorrowful conclusion. "Let's get our table before I start snacking on the bartender."

A little confused about seating two instead of three, the La Petite Grange hostess handed them off to a muscular waiter who introduced himself as Beck. "This way, ladies." He led them through a maze of tables filled with rowdy patrons.

"Is it always this loud?" Gina asked, sitting down.

Beck handed them leather-bound menus. "Only when we host a corporate event. A few weeks ago, we hosted the Baptist convention. After the first glass of wine, everyone loses their religion." He winked. "Now, what are you ladies having to drink?"

Food and drinks came out quickly and their basket of rosemary-olive bread was constantly refilled. After devouring her crab cake entree, Gina checked her watch. "Do you think she's going to make it?"

"She better, since this was her idea." Shanice picked at her over-cooked lasagna. "It must be killing her that we are out together. She thinks of you as the one who got away."

"If we'd gone out, I'd be one of her burnt-out exes."

"I wish she would stop rolling her eyes every time I say more than two sentences to you."

Gina laughed. "And you catch an attitude whenever Officer Childress visits. She does look nice in that uniform."

"I can wear a uniform. Frisk you, if that's what you like."

The comment hung there unacknowledged. Feeling awkward and embarrassed, Shanice looked around the partially enclosed dining room. There were several fire pits to accommodate the people seated outdoors. Beyond the restaurant was an open plaza with decorated archways and a fountain simulating a waterfall – the perfect backdrop for a wedding. "If Ms. Barbara and Lisa had dinner here, it had to be for convenience. It must be beautiful when the sky is clear, but the food isn't particularly good."

"If it's half as busy as it is tonight, no one with a camera would look out of place." Gina pointed toward a table where a tipsy young man was trying to corral his friends into a group photo.

Shanice shoved the plate away and Beck materialized at her side. "You're passing on dessert, right?" Before either could respond, he slid a tray with the check and breath mints on the table. "Have a great night!"

The line behind the hostess desk had mushroomed. Gina signed the bill to the room. "I'm tired of this crowd. Let's order dessert via room service."

Twisting and turning to avoid wayward drinks, they made their way back into the lobby. Thankfully, they were alone in the elevator. "That's not the spot for a quiet, romantic dinner," Shanice said. "How did watching the employees go?"

"I didn't know what to look for. They looked like regular, overworked people. I didn't catch anyone taking pictures on the sly. I did learn something about Barbara, though."

"Seriously? What did you find out?"

Gina stopped at a door and swiped her cardkey. "I'll tell you when Debra gets here."

Walking into the room, they found Debra sitting on the bed watching TV. "Tell me what?"

Because exotic ingredients took time to procure and prepare, the Chopin Cart required seventy-two-hour notice to cater an event. No exceptions, unless you were the wife of a senator who woke up from a martini marathon and remembered that she was hosting a fundraiser for the arts council in the morning.

Debra had one foot out of the door when she was paged through the store's intercom. Did anyone care that she had plans for the night? No, she needed to corral the others and assemble enough crust-less cucumber sandwiches, prosciutto-roasted pepper bites, and mini-shrimp salad cups for a hundred people. After all the food was packed and stacked for morning delivery, the in-house pizzeria rewarded them with a buffet in the employees' break room.

When the cab dropped Debra in front of the Bitmore-Key, more food was the last thing she wanted. She spotted Gina and Shanice having dinner but had no interest in wading through the chaotic scene to get to them. Instead, she took out her phone and, without drawing too much attention to herself, began to film them. The pang of jealousy she felt when they leaned in to talk was obliterated by cheers and hisses from the sports fans at the bar.

What Debra really wanted to do was kick off her shoes, loosen her belt, and relax. That was when the idea came to her – could she get into Gina's room without a key? She moved to the end of the short but slow-moving line at the front desk. Could she get away with it when she didn't even know what floor Gina was on?

The woman in front of her, trying to balance an armload of shopping bags, was having the same problem. "I didn't lose the key; it's right here." She tossed the gray plastic card on the counter. "It's been demagnetized somehow; I can't get back in the room."

Monica, the clerk on duty, took the card and slid it through an unseen mechanism. "Ma'am, I am sorry that happened; the cards can be finicky next to cell phones. Unfortunately, I can't issue you another key because you aren't registered to the room. We can give Mr. Ballard another key or he can add you as a room guest." Debra frowned. She could cross this approach from the list.

The blond head wobbled furiously. "Ronald is in the middle of a business meeting. I don't know which conference room he's in." She twisted her neck to peer into the doorway behind the counter. "Where's Paul? He checked us in, he can vouch for me –"

After a few more tense moments, the key-less shopper hauled her treasures to a corner. The desk clerk beckoned Debra forward. "How can I help you?" she asked, her smile never waning.

Drawing on her days in the high school drama club, Debra put the phone to her ear and sighed. "What do you want, Steve? No, we don't have a problem; you do," she said tersely. "I bought that expensive-as-hell organic fruit and the specialty flour – you need to make those damn pies." She put a hand over the phone and leaned toward the clerk. "Can you have housekeeping send an extra set of towels to my room?"

"Not a problem at all," Monica replied. "Your name and room number?"

Debra put the phone back to her ear and rolled her eyes. "I don't care how tired you are. Make a pot of coffee." She turned and took a few baby steps away. "Gina Smallwood," she said over her shoulder. Though she continued to sigh and fuss into the phone, it was her turn to listen intently.

"Room 652 needs an extra set of towels."

"That's how I found out what room you were in," Debra explained. "I walked in right behind the housekeeper."

Gina was stunned. "She didn't question you at all?"

"I had my Chopin advantage card out as if I was ready to swipe, so I looked legit. She put the towels in the bathroom and went on her way."

Agitated, Gina began pacing. "That's completely unacceptable. You pay for a room, the least the hotel can do is not open your door for strangers. That clerk and housekeeper need to be fired. I'm going to report them." She reached for the telephone.

Debra and Shanice exchanged a look. "Wait, Gina. I frightened that little Filipino lady half to death when I walked in."

"Then she should have called security."

"It's not that serious," Debra insisted.

"When was the first time you walked into your space and found someone standing there uninvited?"

Shanice spoke up. "Gina, if you complain about the hotel staff, the manager will probably have Debra arrested. You can't complain that someone should have alerted security and then expect them not to do it."

"Arrested? For what?"

"Trespassing, fraud, impersonating you. Attempted burglary."

"Fine, I'll let it go." Gina crossed her arms and sat on the bed. "Cynthia had more of an impact on me than I wanted to admit."

"I'm sorry," Debra said. "I didn't mean to make you feel that way. When the idea popped into my head, I didn't think about any consequences. On top of everything else, I destroyed my own theory that it had to be an employee. Anyone devious enough could have tricked their way in."

Gina raised her hands. "No more," she said. "I don't feel like hearing about pictures, murder, or anything else tonight."

Shanice touched her shoulder. "You won't hear about it again. I told you I'm through playing detective. I talked it over with Pastor Robinson and he agreed that I should concentrate on building the church website, including a tribute to Ms. Barbara."

"For real?" Debra asked.

Shanice grinned. "Yep, I'm actually getting back to my chosen profession. I'll need pictures, archival footage. I'm going to be spending all my time in front of my laptop."

"That's something I can help you with," Gina said. "I know the guys on the audio/video team."

Debra was looking away, distant. "Hey," Shanice said, "can I borrow your video camera? I'm going to set up a confessional type room where people can share their stories and memories."

"No way," Debra said. "My camera isn't getting passed around by a bunch of strangers. Everybody in church ain't righteous and – funeral or not – it would disappear. I'll do the filming."

Gina smiled. "So all three of us are going to church? The building might fall. Do you two even own dresses?"

Debra's eyes widened. "No one said anything about wearing a dress."

"The saints aren't going to talk to you if you don't look sanctified. The funeral isn't until Wednesday; you have plenty of time to sanctify your wardrobe. Now get out of here; I'm ready for a hot shower and a good night's sleep." Ignoring their protests, Gina ushered them out and slid the dead bolt into place.

Chapter 24

As they walked down the winding pathway to the guest parking lot, Debra was adamant about not violating her personal dress code. "Neither of my dresses are appropriate for church and I'm not buying a new one either."

"Dress pants are fine. Everyone will be focused on the funeral, not us." Shanice put the key in the ignition and the car sputtered before roaring to life.

Debra drew the seatbelt tight across her chest. "I had no idea Gina was that upset. Sorry I even suggested coming out here."

"How could you know? We were in shock last night and didn't really have a chance to talk about it."

On the highway, a gray and white Ford played a lethargic hopscotch with the lanes. Brake lights on the cars traveling in the cluster around it flickered like a pinball machine. Was he drunk, from out of town, or both? One by one, the other drivers accelerated to swerve around it. When her chance came, Shanice surged by.

"It will be over soon," Debra said. "The news finally revealed that the police have a person of interest. Childress' drifter is on the verge of being charged."

"Arresting him would be a waste of time."

"How would you know? There something you aren't telling me? Spill it!"

Shanice glanced over at Debra before refocusing on the road ahead. Seeing Gina scared and vulnerable left her agitated. "Why? So you can slip information to your new girlfriend?"

"I would never have invited Cynthia in if I knew what she was really up to." Folding her arms tightly across her chest, Debra shielded her embarrassment with anger. "Even if she were, I know how to keep a secret."

"Right," Shanice said. "So you brought up my visit to Renee in front of Gina on purpose? 'Open robes and cinnamon rolls.' You couldn't wait to run your mouth."

"That was an accident. I got caught up in the moment." Debra sucked her teeth and sighed heavily. "I should have taken a cab back."

"Maybe you should have."

After a few miles of silence, Debra broke down. "I'm sorry. Honestly, it was unintentional. I didn't plan for that to happen. But this thing with Gina aside, we've been friends for years –"

A high beam in the rearview mirror caught Shanice's attention. It was the Ford coming up fast. She slid over to the right lane, hoping he would pass by; instead, he followed her. Gripping the steering wheel, she fought back panic. They should take a picture of the car and the license plate, just in case something happened. She was going to interrupt Debra's monologue when the Ford took an exit ramp and disappeared into the city.

Oblivious to the drama unfolding on the driver's side, Debra continued making her case. "…the skeletons in my closet, under my bed, buried in the backyard. You can talk to me about it."

Shanice sighed. Why should she suffer alone? "Your suspect was already in jail when the killer left a note on my car."

"What!"

As they sped along the interstate, Shanice explained everything from discovering the flier on the car in front of New Life Sanctuary to watching Pastor Robinson feed it to the shredder. "I'm supposed to build the website and forget everything else."

Debra couldn't believe it. "Did you call Childress?"

"Are you kidding? No note means no evidence."

"If the pastor goes to the police first, you're going to be in trouble."

"He's not going to say anything."

"I bet he's the killer. He put the note on your car to scare you off and justify stopping the investigation."

"Doesn't make sense," Shanice said. "I was ready to give up after I hit a dead end with Renee. He begged me to continue."

"Exactly!" Debra slapped the dashboard. "His wife is dead and he cares more about finding a photographer than finding her killer?"

At the next red light, Shanice turned to face her roommate. "Did you just change theories midstream? Why would Pastor Robinson ask me to keep looking when I was ready to quit if he didn't want me to find anything?"

"It's simple. Robinson used you to test how good he's been at covering his tracks. You got too close. Now the mysterious note appears and disappears." Debra clasped her hands. "He did it."

"He couldn't have put the note on my car. He didn't know where I was going to be and has barely been alone for more than five minutes since the murder."

"Maybe he has an accomplice. I know you cleared Lisa, but she could be a really good actress."

"Okay, that's enough. You've had five theories in the last thirty seconds." Shanice did wonder at the possibility of Oliver shadowing her but decided not to mention him at all. Besides, he wasn't the kind of person who disappeared into a crowd. "The photographer and the killer are likely the same person. I am pretty sure a member of the church is involved. It wasn't an outsider who put the envelope on Pastor Robinson's desk."

Debra's imagination flourished. "A member of Hope Reborn walked into the annex house, bashed Barbara Robinson's skull in, calmly walked back into the sanctuary, and slipped into a pew?"

Shanice cringed as an image of the crime scene flashed through her mind. "The blood – it was everywhere. How can you walk out into the street a bloody mess and no one notice? That's the question."

Chapter 25

Gina woke up feeling refreshed. The honey bourbon tea from room service had settled her nerves and ushered her into a peaceful sleep. Now, full of scrambled eggs and toast, she sipped on her second cup of coffee while watching the sunlight shimmering off the lake.

The fiasco last night wasn't anyone's fault. Hotel staff being courteous wasn't incompetence. The stunt was a reminder that no one was ever safe.

That reminded Gina, she had meant to tell her housemates that Ms. Barbara was a regular guest at L'Aurore. Between her time in the sauna and the massage table, she overheard staff sharing their memories of her.

She couldn't imagine Ms. Barbara enjoying spa services. Unlike other ministerial couples, the Robinsons never wore their prosperity. Everyone knew Ms. Barbara made sure they adhered to a frugal lifestyle. Could this be the same woman who enjoyed a pricey, head-to-toe seaweed wrap?

Her interest piqued, Gina decided to probe for a bit more information about Ms. Barbara as a client. She wasn't investigating; she was curious for another perspective of the authority figure she grew up with.

She checked out and dropped her overnight bag with the bell captain before going to L'Aurore.

Robin, the manicurist, showed Gina into a small but vigorously ventilated room where rows of nail polish appeared embedded in the walls. After pouring them each a glass of citrus-infused water, she praised her client's soft hands and set to work.

Almost immediately, Robin began asking the "care" questions. Gina had seen her cousin do it countless times in her beauty shop. It was lighthearted banter designed to make the customer feel more at ease. They talked about briefly about Gina's job and discovered they had grown up in adjacent neighborhoods.

Finally, Robin asked, "Doing anything special this week?"

It was an awkward opening, but Gina took it. "I'm going to a funeral."

The manicurist's face fell. "Oh, I'm so sorry."

"It's terrible what happened. You may have heard about her? Barbara Robinson?"

Robin's head bobbed up and down enthusiastically. "Miss Barbara was one of my clients. She used to come here every other month with her friend Ms. Dorothy. It was like a girls' day out. They got massages, a mani-pedi, had dinner. You know, they treated themselves."

"Really?"

Robin leaned in a little closer and lowered her voice. "As a minister's wife, Ms. Barbara felt like she couldn't do a bold color on her hands. They were usually a soft pink or clear. Her toes were a different story. Peach, Metallic Plumb, Tangerine Sunrise – it was always a color that matched one of her multicolored scarfs. One day, she walked out of here with Raspberry Risk."

Gina gasped in mock horror. "Scandalous!" She understood Ms. Barbara's plight. Nail polish was one of the imaginary sins that agitated the church mothers. "Had she been here recently?"

"She stopped coming regularly after Ms. Dorothy passed. It was like she lost a sister, you know? A few weeks ago, she came back with a niece, but it wasn't the same." Robin's eyes began to tear. "Ms. Barbara actually helped me avoid a disaster."

Gina retracted her hands slowly. She didn't want someone who was upset attacking her cuticles. "What happened?"

"When I got engaged, I came to work flashing my ring and everyone was ecstatic. Ms. Barbara took me aside and asked if I was ready for that kind of commitment. She said, 'If you treat love like it's scarce, everything you do to keep it will be an act of desperation.' The woman read me like a book."

"Ms. Barbara was pretty blunt."

"I said it's what I wanted. My younger sisters had already gone down the aisle, bought houses, and had children. It was finally my turn." Robin sighed. "I went home and cried. The truth is I didn't want a husband; I wanted the honeymoon trip to the Cayman Islands."

"Wow."

"Yeah. I called it off before the official invitations went out and booked a solo trip. I'm not sure if I would have gone through with marrying Richie, but I'm glad Ms. Barbara forced me to think about it."

They silently reflected on broken engagements while Robin painted Gina's nails in Plumb Perfection.

Chapter 26

The weekend had gone by too quickly. Shanice spent most of the time in her pajamas, curled up in front of a television. Though she wanted to relax, her thoughts often strayed back to murder, gossip, and closeted Christians. Occasionally, she looked out at her car to make sure no new notes appeared on the windshield.

It took a lot of sleep and Blaxploitation films to put her mind at ease. The tension in her shoulders had unfurled by Wednesday morning. She would go to the funeral clear-headed and attentive – if she could find parking.

Two blocks downhill of Hope Reborn Baptist Church, Shanice maneuvered the car into the only legal spot available. While she concentrated on not tapping the sports car behind them, Gina finished another re-telling of a story she had become obsessed with – Barbara Robinson's closed-toe secret. "You guys don't understand how radical this is. This Ms. Barbara sounds nothing like my Sunday school teacher."

Debra scoffed from the back seat. The blazer hugging her shoulders made her feel like a sausage. "A religious hypocrite? What else is new?"

"That's not really fair," Gina said. "Ms. Barbara never shamed us about the way our hair or nails were done. Growing up, I lumped all the elders together. I would have liked her if I got the chance to know her as an adult."

"Church is like the club," Debra said. "It's hard to get to know people there because everyone is wearing a mask."

"If you feel that way about the club, why do you still go?"

Gina twisted around in her seat to see the response.

Debra laughed. "The two-for-one drink specials. Seriously, not that many other places to meet women offline."

Satisfied that no one would be able to box her in, Shanice cut the ignition. "There's no reason you can't meet a woman in church," she teased.

"Don't be fooled by the quiet demeanor," Gina added as she touched up her makeup. "Sanctified on Sunday; sinful on Saturday."

The mood changed as they joined the informal procession of people trekking up the hill.

Near the entrance, an usher corralled news media behind a rope barrier. In her crisp uniform, she insisted that reporters adhere to the rules. "No video cameras are allowed inside. You cannot block the door; that is a fire hazard. If people want to talk to you, they will come over to you."

A town car pulled up alongside the hearse. As if to underscore her point, the older gentleman who emerged peeked over his sunglasses at those assembled and was drawn to a cameraman.

The reporters occupied for the moment, the usher whipped around to see the approaching trio. She wagged a finger at Debra's camera and pointed to the chaos behind the barricade. "I'm sorry, sisters, it's the viper pit for you."

Gina stepped forward. "Sister Jameson, we aren't the press. We're here to help Pastor Robinson with the memorial."

Frustrated wrinkles fell away from the usher's face as her eyes widened. "Wait, you're one of the Smallwood girls, right? Gina? Girl, I ain't seen you in a month of Sundays. How have you been? Still in school. No, your aunt said you had graduated?"

Gina let herself be drawn into the woman's arms. "Finished college and got a job."

"Climbing that corporate ladder? Go on, girl." The usher cleared her throat. "Where you been? Shame it takes something like this to bring you back to your church home."

"I may not go to church, but I still go to God."

"Can't argue with that. I think the web people are supposed to set up in the changing room, but Sarah knows all about that. Last time I saw her, she was headed to the sanctuary. It's so good to see you again, darling." Sister Jameson gave Gina's hand one final squeeze before moving out of the way.

Once through the double glass doors, Shanice exhaled. "You handled that like a pro."

"Ahem, I am a pro." Gina snapped her fingers. "You let Sarah know that you are here. I'll take Debra to the changing room; it's right across the vestibule, the little room next to the baptismal pool."

"You aren't coming upstairs?" Shanice asked.

"No," Gina said quietly. "I'm not ready to view the body yet."

Another group walked in, crowding the small entryway. Debra huffed and pulled her equipment closer. "Let's get this over with."

As she climbed the steps to the sanctuary, Shanice felt a tightness in her chest. She was never supposed to be alone. The killer could be at the funeral too. She was to go about her business doing the work of getting personal stories while Debra carefully watched those around her. They planned to do this without signaling to Gina that something was wrong. Now, despite their plans, they were easily separated.

The usher at the sanctuary door handed out programs bearing the image of a much younger Barbara Robinson. Her smile was crooked, but the arm holding her purse was bone straight. She looked like a commander marshaling troops with no doubt of her impending victory.

The size of the sanctuary surprised Shanice. The church's public access show focused exclusively on the altar and choir stands. She did not expect the many stained glass windows depicting miracles or the rows and rows of gleaming mahogany pews.

The line to view the body extended halfway down the center aisle, obscuring most of the coffin from view. Shanice wasn't ready to see the body either. Though it was early, the pews were starting to fill with mourners. Sarah was sitting in the choir stand, rubbing the shoulders of a distraught young man. Through the force of a stare, Shanice tried to catch her attention. If Sarah could just look up and acknowledge her with a nod, she could be on her way.

"Hi!"

Shanice looked down. It was the little girl that she had saved from a horrifying Sunday school lesson. "You have to sign the guest book first," she whispered through her fingers before pointing it out. Then, "That's my grandma," she said before skip-walking toward an elderly woman with a creased brow.

Knowing her own grandmother would think it rude to show up at a funeral and not have the decency to view the body, Shanice decided adding her name to the list of visitors would be a good compromise. Two women standing near the registry were clearly upset. Pretending to concentrate on her penmanship, Shanice listened intently.

"Whose idea was it to set aside pews for so-called important people? This isn't a political rally; it's a funeral."

"It's not what Ms. Barbara would have wanted. How you gonna honor her by doing something she would disapprove of?"

"Humph! I imagine a lot of things are about to happen that Ms. Barbara wouldn't like."

"You see how that one's been acting around pastor? Can hardly wait to get his wife in the ground."

"Do me a favor. You ever see me lose commonsense over a man, pull my coattail. Don't let me embarrass myself like that old fool."

Shanice wondered who they were talking about. Straightening up, she meant to cast a nonchalant glance around the sanctuary; suddenly, she remembered another favor.

Cheryl got to church late because she did a favor for someone. Deaconess Ophelia. She arrived at church early that day and disappeared. What was so important that she passed her sick and shut-in duties on to someone else?

Deciding that her chat with Sarah could wait, Shanice went back to the usher. "Excuse me, I need to find Deaconess Ophelia, but I've never met her before. Is she in the sanctuary?"

The answer came with a nod to the left side of the church. "Sitting in the first pew, black and white hat."

In her early 30s, the woman was younger than Shanice expected. She didn't look matronly, but her dark gray dress extended past her knees. "Hi, Ophelia? My name is Shanice Wilkins."

A soft, round face tilted up to meet her gaze. Confusion gave way to a smile. "The new webmaster. I saw you at Rev Robinson's house. Do you need something?"

"Yes." Thankful that no one was sitting near, Shanice slid into the pew next to her. "I was with Rev Robinson when he found Ms. Barbara. You were at the church that morning; did you see anything unusual? The police won't tell me anything, but I need to know what happened."

"Oh, baby, I understand." Ophelia dabbed her wet, puffy eyes with tissue. "Unfortunately, I can't help you. I was asleep in the ladies' lounge when they found Ms. Barbara. I woke up when a group of girls came in crying. They told me what happened."

Shanice tried again. "What about when you saw Deaconess Cheryl? Was anyone else here?"

Ophelia shrugged. "Plenty of folks were around, but I don't remember who. I worked a double shift the night before. Could barely keep my eyes open. Seeing Cheryl in the parking lot was a blessing. She hadn't even cut the engine. I passed the communion kit on to her and went straight to the lounge."

Shanice felt a hand on her shoulder. Turning around, she

faced a harried Sarah. "I'm glad you're here early. We need to go over some of the logistics before you set up."

The walk to the secretary's office was full of pleasantries and small talk. Once Sarah closed the door, her passive demeanor changed. "Okay, what's your scam?"

"Scam?"

"You're the so-called professional, right? How are you going to walk in here without any equipment to film the tribute messages? You going to record them on that ancient flip phone trying to fight its way out of your back pocket? There are going to be hundreds of people here – how many low res grainy videos you think will fit on the memory card?"

Shanice self-consciously pat the phone in her back pocket. "Wait, let me explain –"

"You gave Pastor Robinson some hard luck story so that he would hire you. Fine. Maybe you didn't intend to get in over your head. But Ms. Barbara is dead. This is too serious for you to half-ass your way through it. She deserves better than that."

"My camera woman is setting up in the baptismal changing room," Shanice said. "She's using a digital video recorder that captures every detail, right down to the pores. I know this is a stressful time for you, but don't take it out on me because you can't yell at a deacon."

"I'm sorry." Sarah deflated as she sat down. "So far, anything that can go wrong has and everyone expects me to fix it. If Ms. Barbara were here, she would tell people to solve their own problems. I can't do that."

"I do understand. Have you had a chance to rest at all?"

"No. I know she's gone, but there hasn't been a moment to be by myself, to grieve. What has it been like for you, finding her and all?"

"I try not to dwell on it. This project is going to be good for me too; I'd like to block that image out with the good memories of her friends."

"There are going to be a lot of memories," Sarah said.

"There's an announcement on the back of the program and I'm going to mention it during service. We'll tell people that they can stop by during the repast and to limit themselves to three minutes."

Shanice found the announcement and discovered it included her email address. Before she could ask, Sarah continued, "I included your email because I thought people who are camera shy could at least write a few words of remembrance."

A loud noise startled both of them. Cracking the office door, Shanice saw a familiar woman storming across the vestibule. "Do you know that woman?"

Sarah nudged Shanice aside and cast a disapproving glance at the troublemaker's back. "That's Trina. She comes off and on, but she's not a member."

"That's not her name," Shanice said as they watched Cynthia "Ceeda Truth" Tavares disappear into a room.

Chapter 27

The preparation room for baptism candidates was empty except for a clothing rack and three folding chairs. A tapestry depicting a brown-haired Jesus with open arms hid the staircase leading up to the adjacent baptismal pool. Soft fluorescent light from overhead fixtures reflected off the sea-foam blue walls, evoking a feeling of tranquility.

Debra considered using The Good Shepherd as a backdrop. Dismissing the idea, she arranged the chairs to avoid visual distractions. As she adjusted the camera lens, the door flew open and Cynthia walked into the frame. "Hey, get out of here!"

Cynthia raised her hands defensively. "I want to apologize." The soft-spoken, eye-fluttering nymph was back. "When I'm after a story, sometimes I stir things up to see what shakes out. I went over the line with you."

Debra was angry. Dimples and a tight dress weren't going to work this time. "You lied your way into our house and then tried to extort us."

"They were empty threats. I was trying to push Shanice to come clean. Following her around got me nowhere."

"There was nothing to come clean about!"

"I know that now. I did a little more checking into her background." The smile couldn't hide the sarcasm in her tone. "It's unlikely that the former treasurer of the Spectra Alliance is anywhere near the pastor's inner circle."

"Whatever it takes, huh? A lie here and there, nasty notes, anonymous phone calls. Anything to fill up your column."

"I've done all that and more. I've got a job to do."

"Get out of here. Officer Childress told you to stay away from us."

"I have every right to be here; this funeral is a public event."

"Get out of this room."

Ignoring the command, Cynthia sat down. "Let's keep this civil. I need to talk to your friend Gina. As a long time member, she has to know what's happening behind the scenes."

"Why don't you join the church and figure it out for yourself?"

"I've been to a few services here." Cynthia sucked her teeth. "The lady in charge of the clothing ministry keeps the nicer things for herself. There's a deacon who takes more money out of the collection plate than he puts in. I've got nothing about Pastor Robinson beyond the usual infidelity rumors. I can't even find credible proof of that."

Debra remembered a column where Ceeda bragged about the ministers she tempted into sin. "You tried to seduce him, didn't you? It didn't go well?"

"He shook my hand and kept it moving. Mrs. Robinson pulled me aside and advised me not to be so forward in presenting myself. She said I should concentrate on Jesus and a husband of my own would come in due time."

The small room could hardly contain Debra's laughter. "I'm sure half of her job was to put women like you in their place."

"Barbara Robinson was direct; I liked her."

"Yet, here you are, at her funeral, trying to dig up dirt on her husband." Debra opened the door. "This space is to honor her, so please leave."

Cynthia rolled her eyes before exiting.

Debra leaned against the closed door and exhaled loudly. The Jesus curtain parted and Shanice emerged with another woman. "What the hell. Is someone going to rappel down from the ceiling next? How did you get back there?"

"There's more than one way to the baptismal pool," Shanice said. "This is Sarah."

The secretary pointed at the door. "That woman is a reporter?"

Debra looked to her friend for guidance. When Shanice nodded, she let the truth fly. "Cynthia writes for the *Edmondson Enquirer* under the name Ceeda Truth."

Sarah's hands drew up into tight fists. "The gossip columnist who's been spreading those lies about ministers? She won't be able to step inside a church when I get through." She turned to Shanice. "Looks like you're all set up here. Again, sorry I gave you a hassle earlier. Excuse me."

After Sarah left, Debra unbuttoned her vest and rolled back her sleeves. She felt as if she'd worked a full day and was ready to go home. "How much did you hear?"

"Enough." Shanice sat down and closed her eyes. She jumped up again. "Where's Gina?"

"I sent her to find you," Debra said. "I didn't want you out there alone."

"If Cynthia finds her first, we might have a double funeral."

Chapter 28

Gina did not recognize Charles Pruitt. She walked onto the balcony expecting the skinny, awkward kid with over-sized glasses who never had enough money to buy what he wanted from the corner store.

"Gina Misdemeanor," he said. Not only had Charles gotten taller, his voice had dropped two octaves, and she could see his muscles through his suit.

"Chuck-A-Buck," she responded. "Always down on his luck."

He straightened out his tie and patted his fresh haircut. "They call me Charlie now. It's good to see you, despite the circumstances."

Gina looked at the cameras and other equipment positioned in the first row. "You're recording tonight?"

"Yeah. I wanted to do a live stream, but Pops doesn't like anything to go up unedited."

"Live stream? No more VHS tapes?"

He smiled. "Where you been at? We switched to DVDs years ago. When Mother Xavier started talking about recording her soaps on DVR, Pops knew it was time to upgrade. Next stop, Video On Demand." He adjusted the color on one of the monitors. "Do you think the new website will have an e-commerce component?"

Gina crossed her arms. "What makes you think I have anything to do with that?" Charles tilted his head and raised an eyebrow. They both laughed. The Hope Reborn grapevine moved at lightning speed. "It depends on what the church is willing to pay for. Speaking of content, do you think we can get a few video clips for the website memorial? From the earliest recorded services to today – a few scenes featuring Ms. Barbara."

Looking down at the altar, Gina had a flashback to the days when she and her friends would disappear to the balcony to exchange stories and candy. Edward Pruitt, Charles' father, wore huge headphones that looked like a helmet; he'd be so focused on recording that he paid them no mind. Ms. Barbara would cast her eyes to the balcony before reminding parents they should always know what their children were doing.

Gina felt a wave of sadness. "Remember how she would know we were up here, even when we tried to hide?"

Charles laughed. "Don't care what anybody else says, she had x-ray vision. I dropped a couple of marbles once and the sound reverberated throughout the building. Dad believed me when I told him it was change that fell from my pocket. Ms. Barbara didn't buy that for a minute and for the next month made me empty my pockets before Sunday school. She got my marbles, Legos, gum – anything I was trying to sneak in."

"When she confiscated my candy, I fell back on the peppermints in my mother's purse."

"Let's get back to talking about the future," Charles said. "We'll need VOD capabilities on the website. Until then, we'd want to sell compilation DVDs. I'm thinking we can center sales around themes like He Is Risen: The Best of Easter Sunday or Pastor Robinson's Revelations About Revelations. We could even do a box set of the seven deadly sins. We have years of content that can be re-purposed and monetized. Pops doesn't believe in my vision, though."

"That's because your vision tends to be limited," a husky voice said from behind. Edward Pruitt had lost the weight that his son had gained but was still the picture of elegance. Bending down to kiss Gina on the cheek, he smelled like cigars. "How you been doing, gal?"

"Fine, Mr. Pruitt. How about yourself?"

"I got more hairs on my chin than on my head now, but I can't complain." Mr. Pruitt pointed towards his son. "This one went to college and came out talking like a marketing executive."

Charles' face tightened. "All I want to do is turn Pruitt Video into Pruitt Digital Imaging."

Mr. Pruitt waved dismissively. "The last time Chuck told me he had a vision, I let him do a Sunday service all on his own. I thought it would be nice to be in the audience for a change. Sat down to watch it afterward and this boy had zoomed in on all the breasts that he could find."

"I was nineteen!"

The old videographer winked at Gina and continued. "Didn't matter if it was a low-cut dress on the choir stand or a grandmotherly bounty. Chuck didn't have a preference; just bosoms bouncing everywhere." He looked at Charles. "Stop pouting, boy. Go outside and let the reporters know that we will make footage available to them after the service. Hand out business cards and do that thing where you talk like a professional."

Resigned, Charles gave a weak wave to Gina. "Catch up with you later."

Though she tried to remain neutral while the scene unfolded between father and son, Gina took up for her friend after he left. "Mr. Pruitt, his ideas aren't that bad."

"I'm not resistant to change, but Charles isn't mature enough to handle everything yet. For example, he should have more respect for Barbara than to talk about monetizing her content – her life's work – at her own funeral! He has the business sense, but not the common sense. Now, I heard you asking about old footage?"

"Yes, for the memorial section of the web page."

"Charles can put together some highlights for you, but I have two conditions." He held up a leathery index finger. "You'll have to give us full and proper credit."

"That won't be a problem."

Another finger sprang up. "Even with the clips that

Chuck sends, you have to promise me that you won't put anything that would embarrass somebody on the line, on the net. You know what I mean – nothing viral."

"Sir?"

"Charles has shown me those videos of people shouting out of their wigs or doing a vigorous praise dance where everything jiggles. I don't want to find out you put up a clip of Deacon Jeffries wiping his brow and ending up with a handkerchief stained with hair dye."

"Mr. Pruitt, I'd never do something like that to my church family." Gina giggled. Her mother would often whisper about the vain deacon who wore expensive suits but used cheap hair dye.

"Jeffries done got one of those sewn-in things now." Mr. Pruitt cleared his throat. "You can see everything through this lens. People cut their eyes when a certain person passes their aisle. Some people got the fancy clothes and the nice hat but hesitating a little before putting money in the offering plate. People betray themselves all of the time through body language."

Gina knew he wanted to tell her something. Men preferred to think of it as sharing information rather than engaging in gossip. She got up to let him know that he was in danger of losing his audience. "Thank you, Mr. Pruitt. Don't forget to come down after service to record your remembrance of Ms. Barbara. We're asking everyone to talk about a way she touched their lives."

Mr. Pruitt cracked, "You know, half the people boohooing were barely speaking to Barbara Robinson these last few weeks."

"What happened?"

"If Barbara felt you were doing wrong, she'd let you know. Hurt a lot of feelings. She sure did." He smiled to himself; her lectures hadn't been directed at him. "Now you better get downstairs, young lady. The pews are filling up quick!"

Hesitantly peeking around the door, Shanice hoped to avoid Cynthia. The reporter was at the opposite end of the room, cornered by two older women. A crowd gathered around the trio.

As Shanice wound her way through the vestibule, she saw Oliver sitting by himself and cradling a cup in his hands. Sensing something was wrong, she made her way over to him and touched his shoulder. "Hi," she began. " I know you miss her."

Oliver smiled weakly and motioned for her to sit down. "Thank you. I've played at friends' funerals before, but this is very tough. I know her spirit has gone on, but I needed a break from sitting behind the casket."

"Are you okay? Should I get someone?"

"No, I'll be fine for the service." He licked his lower lip and looked down.

Shanice remembered how hard it was to get Pastor Robinson alone. Oliver was dealing with his own grief and the loneliness of having an inaccessible partner. "There's so much happening, you probably haven't had much time together."

"Between her family, people wanting to help, and the police, it's nearly impossible."

"Detective Gerard?"

"Mmhmm. Pops up at random to ask the same questions in slightly different ways. He's around here somewhere." Suddenly, a smile spread across Oliver's face and he stood to greet someone.

Shanice recognized the side profile. "Hi, Renee." She pulled out the chair next to her. "Join us?"

The disappointment in Renee's eyes had no effect on her faux smile. She ignored the invitation and continued hugging Oliver. "How are you, sweetie?"

The pianist gripped the singer's hand. "A little down, but seeing you makes it all better. Your name isn't in the program; was Walter able to reach you? Don't be surprised if he calls you from the audience to sing."

Renee leaned into him. "You know I'm always prepared. Barbara's sister called me."

He gave her another squeeze. "Wonderful." Oliver looked at his watch. "Let me get back to my post. See you in a few." He patted Shanice's shoulder before walking off.

Before Renee could leave, Shanice tugged her arm. "Hold on, I do need to talk to you for a minute." Her ex looked around anxiously. "Don't worry; if anyone asks, I'll pretend we just met."

"Fine." Renee sat. "What is it?"

"Do you recognize her?" She pointed out a scowling Cynthia, who angrily jabbed at her phone. "Do you recognize her?"

"I think her name is Trina. She came to the studio once for the free evaluation. Total waste of time."

"In what way?"

Renee thought for a moment. "She has an okay voice, but she wasn't really interested in lessons. She kept asking weird questions about the different churches I sang in. It was awkward. She tried to schedule a full session, but I got rid of her."

"This was when Lisa was still coming to class?" Shanice asked.

"Yeah. She a friend of yours?"

Her suspicions confirmed, Shanice smiled. "That's the woman who scared away your star pupil."

Chapter 29

Sitting on a packed pew between Gina and Ms. Ella, Shanice cried softly. The people around her wore solemn expressions of grief, but her tears came from relief: she wasn't being stalked by a killer.

The calls to Lisa, the photographs, the note on her car – all were attempts by Cynthia to stir up trouble. After attending Hope Reborn without finding any noteworthy scandal, the gossip switched her approach from honey to vinegar.

There had been no demand for money because the pictures were supposed to frighten the Robinsons into exposing a "real" scandal. Thanks to bad timing, the Robinsons assumed they came from Renee. Barbara's last days were spent worried about a nonexistent threat.

During the final viewing and expression of condolences, Shanice had tried to signal to Pastor Robinson that the mystery was solved. He had nothing to fear. She took his hands in hers and whispered, "It's okay. Everything is all right." Hopefully, Barbara's soul knew the truth.

Lost in her own thoughts, Shanice did not hear her name being called. With a nudge from Gina, she looked up to see Sarah at the front of the altar. "Shanice?" Sarah asked, "Are you here?"

Shanice stood up and the secretary continued. "Ms. Wilkins and her team are recording your most cherished memories of our beloved First Lady. They are set up in the room adjacent to the baptism pool and I believe someone is there now?" Sarah waited for a nod before continuing.

"Yes. So, if you have a few minutes, the opportunity to share thoughts about Ms. Barbara is available to you."

After more announcements and tributes from various groups and clubs, Renee stood beside the closed casket and gave a heartrending version of "Amazing Grace." Then she re-centered herself, nodded to Oliver, and launched into "Goin' Up Yonder." The energy of the congregation changed from sadness to celebration as they sang along.

The mood shifted again when Pastor Robinson appeared in the pulpit. Though visibly tired, his voice had found its timbre. "First, I'd like to thank everyone for your love and support. When Barbara and I heeded the call to build Hope Reborn, we had no idea all of the blessings this work would bestow upon us."

He paused to straighten out the microphone. "For the young people in the room – and by that I mean anyone under the age of thirty-five – Barbara always referred to you as her babies behind closed doors. When friends wondered why we didn't have biological children, she'd say, 'I already have my hands full with my babies.' Undoubtedly, everyone she mentored knew they were loved.

"Barbara and I had a true partnership. When I couldn't see my way around a situation or the stress of everyday living bore down on me, she helped guide me through. When I was full of despair, she could see and call forth the part of God that is inside of me. I did the same for her. That's what a relationship is. God spoke to me through Barbara."

Pastor Robinson leaned against the podium, his voice dropped low. "How do you think we survived the hardships, the rumors, the misguided attempts at temptation? It's not easy being the First Lady of the Church."

The "amen" erupting from her mother surprised Gina.

"Barbara wanted so much for us as a community. She'd say, 'What good is it to cling to an Old Testament mentality in a New Testament world?' I'm not going to be up here much longer, but I do want to share two of her favorite verses with you. They are printed on the back of your program."

He led the crowd in a reading of Galatians 5:6 and 1 Corinthians 13:13. "For in Christ Jesus, neither circumcision nor uncircumcision means anything, but faith working through love. But now faith, hope, love, abide these three; but the greatest of these is love."

After a moment of reflection, Pastor Robinson continued, "Barbara tried to look at everything from the prism of faith, hope, and, most importantly, love. Love is the greatest and the hardest because it requires us to be vulnerable with each other. It involves risk, taking a chance. Whenever we faced an issue or a situation, the solution had to come from a place of love. Not judgment, scorn, or shame. Love.

"If your sister is hungry, love requires you to feed her without assessing if the cupboard is bare for an acceptable reason. If a single mother is having trouble, love requires you to drop off some diapers without having to evaluate her situation with the baby's father first. We aren't worthy of God's love but, now that we've been saved by grace, we want to turn around and demand others prove their worthiness to us?" Pastor Robinson stepped back from the podium, shrugged his shoulders, and raised his hands.

Several people leapt to their feet.

After wiping his brow, he brought his voice down to a near whisper. "When Dorothy, Barbara's best friend, revealed that the cancer had spread, it was devastating. Barbara heard the word 'inoperable' and started packing. No one knew how many weeks or months Dorothy had left. It didn't matter.

"I loved Dorothy like a sister and, yet, the thought of losing my wife for an indefinite amount of time bothered me. What about Hope Reborn? What about our home? What about me? She said that God told her to go, so if I had a problem, I needed to take it up with Him. She told me to hire a housekeeper. As for the church, if we aren't building an institution that can go on without us, all of this work is for naught."

Oliver slipped back behind the organ and began playing softly.

"Wife, partner, lover, mother, friend, spiritual warrior, healer – there are not enough words to capture the whole of Barbara's essence. It would be travesty on top of tragedy to use her death as a reason to withdraw from the community, from each other. This is not the time for us to roll up the carpet and hide in our spiritual closets. If your faith isn't working through love, it's not working."

Taking the microphone from the stand, Pastor Robinson walked down to the casket. He wept openly. "Barbara, we celebrate your life. The example you set will lead us into the future."

Chapter 30

It was the not-too-distant sound of the garbage truck that propelled Shanice to scramble out of bed and put on a robe. Barefoot, she ran into the backyard to take the bulging green garbage bags out of the plastic bin and deposit them on the other side of the fence.

"Don't worry," said Mr. Kitsch, "you have plenty of time." He braced himself with his cane before laughing. Their neighbor across the alley; it wasn't the first time he'd seen Shanice racing against the truck. He was dressed for the day with his khaki pants, floral shirt, and a tartan golf cap.

"Good morning," Shanice said. The surge of adrenaline over, she felt lethargy creeping back into her bones.

"We do half of the work for them and they still leave half of the trash in the alley." Mr. Kitchi looked at her over his glasses. "You need to commit to waking up or go back to bed; a body can't serve two masters." He winked and began the trek back to his porch. "Have a good day," he called behind him.

Concentrating on the damp coolness of the grass between her toes, Shanice fought back the curtain of sleep. Last night had worn her out. The line to record a memory for Barbara Robinson had stretched around the vestibule and never seemed to get shorter.

A breeze sent a chill up her pajama pants, shocking her mid-yawn. What had she promised Ms. Barbara's sister? A video tribute on the website and a DVD full of digital memories? Before doing too much work on the website, she really needed to have a discussion with Pastor Robinson about the direction he wanted the site to go in. Services needed to be evaluated and choices needed to be made in terms of design and function.

Shanice smiled as she went inside. It felt good to concentrate on building websites again. Poking through other people's lives left a bad taste in her mouth.

Grabbing a bowl for cereal, she reflected on how the Robinsons voluntarily imprisoned a part of themselves with the goal of leading others. That Renee felt compelled to do the same thing astounded her.

"Earth to Shanice, are you there?" Gina said as she sat at the kitchen table. Her jeans and casual blouse meant a quiet day in the office. "How are you doing? Debra struggled out of here about thirty minutes ago. We left you some coffee, but it's probably cold now."

"You left the essence of coffee. There was barely enough for half of a cup." Shanice stretched out her legs. "I noticed how you disappeared on us last night."

"It was God's will for me not to be anywhere near Cynthia. For a moment, it looked like she was going to approach, but she changed direction when my friends and I gave her the stink eye. Pastor Robinson and Ms. Barbara were nowhere near perfect, but church people don't tell our business to outsiders."

"Our business? You suddenly a church girl again?"

Gina laughed. "No, but when you've had a relationship with someone, you have an urge to defend them. Probably the same thing that made you want to protect Renee."

Shanice ignored the reference to her ex. "Debra told you about our encounter with Cynthia?"

"No, I was hanging out with my old Sunday school crew. Sarah told us about the showdown."

"While we were working hard, you were exchanging phone numbers?"

"Excuse me, I did do some business on your behalf. The church audio/visual team is going to email you some video clips of Ms. Barbara. I worked the crowd making sure people got in line. On top of that, I answered all the questions about who you are and what you were doing."

"All I know is that when I stuck my head out the door, I saw you and a bunch of folk posing for pictures."

Gina found the impromptu photo session on her phone. "I'm sure somebody thought it was distasteful, but the whole group hasn't been together in years. That's Charles, Sarah, Bernard, Valerie, Willa, Scottie, me, and Tannis."

"You look like you're at a G-rated club." Shanice pursed her lips in a mock pose.

"Charles, Sarah, and Bernard are still deep in the church. Chuck and his dad are the audio-visual team. Sarah graduated from Ms. Barbara's star pupil to Pastor Robinson's part time secretary. Bernard is a deacon now. He and his wife Cheryl are all about moving up in the hierarchy. Willa still goes off and on now because she's back living with her folks. The rest of us have escaped Hope Reborn for various reasons.

"But I got everybody's business card. Bernard promised me a great deal on a used car. Tannis runs an antique shop off Route 27; she might be interested in some of Aunt Gloria's old knick-knacks. I told Willa that I know of a couple of jobs about to open up in the nonprofit sector."

Shanice remembered Tannis' recording session. She was one of many women who appeared ready to break out into a storm of tears at any moment. "Last night, everybody talked about Ms. Barbara like she should have been able to disarm her assailant with a look of compassion. Tell me what's missing? Could she do no wrong?"

Gina thought about it for a moment. "Ms. Barbara didn't just solve problems; she looked for them. In her mind, you plug a small leak before it becomes a waterfall. She came off as condescending sometimes. Helping a person who hasn't explicitly asked for help can lead to resentment."

Whenever her well-meaning aunt wanted to share her wisdom, Shanice gave her a minute before finding a reason to get off the phone. Unwanted advice was annoying, but nothing to hurt someone over. She pushed the thought away and refocused on building a website. "I need to thank you and Debra for putting up with all of this craziness, especially Cynthia."

"Did Cynthia really admit to stalking and threatening you?"

"That and more," Shanice said. "That and more. She's not trying to find a story; she trying to create one."

"People like her love exploiting weakness in others but forget they have vulnerabilities too." Gina leaned in and added in a whisper, "Do you think she could have killed Ms. Barbara just to see what would happen next?"

Shanice sighed. "I've thought about that. As a woman obsessed with Pastor Robinson, Cynthia has all the qualities Detective Gerard is looking for in a suspect. When she lost control of the situation here, she backed right off. She attacks with words, not hands. "

"She has more sense than to start a three-against-one fight. I have no trouble believing she would attack someone from behind."

"If that was the case, why is she still trying to dig up dirt on the family?" Shanice shook her head. "Nah, I don't see it."

Gina shrugged. "Still, Detective Gerard should know what she's been up to. Are you going to tell him?"

That was another question Shanice had wrestled with. If Gerard uncovered Cynthia's nasty tricks on his own, everyone could get in trouble. He would reprimand Childress and growl his way into St. James to interview Lisa. The teacher would be fired before the end of the day.

"I think it may come out better if Pastor Robison brings her up. Lisa is the person I need to talk to. The woman has been a wreck for weeks; I'll be happy to put her mind at ease." Shanice thought back on their meeting and winced. "I never got her phone number, so I'll have to go back to her church. That's not going to be fun."

"You should definitely tell her," Gina said, "but don't be surprised if she isn't relieved."

"Why wouldn't she be?"

"If I were Lisa, I'd have questions. For example, of all the people Ms. Barbara knew, why did Cynthia target me? How did a tabloid hack get my phone number?" Gina bristled. "With the school always looking over my shoulder, I wouldn't feel safe at all."

Chapter 31

Half a day into the memorial project, Shanice felt mired in quicksand. Thanks to Gina's efforts, she had over four hours of footage to whittle down into a short video. Interviewees often talked beyond the three-minute limit and ignored persistent but gentle prompts to get to the point. The media editing software on Debra's laptop had more options than an amateur could ever need. The jargon-filled tutorials only made her feel stupid.

Acquiescing to Ann-Louise's request marked the second time Shanice agreed to provide a service she wasn't qualified to perform. She should have suggested it was a project for Hope Reborn's own audio/video people.

When Debra called during her lunch break, she heard all of Shanice's fears and frustrations. "Cut yourself some slack," the deli manager said. "The woman caught you off-guard and you were in shock from that note. Do what you can. I'll smooth out the rough edges."

"Thanks, I'm a mess." Shanice slumped down in her seat.

Debra yawned. "We'll both feel better after a good night's sleep. On the other hand, you're having a better day than Cynthia. People are leaving comments all over her Ceeda Truth articles that reveal her real name and her dirty tactics. Those good Christian folks are giving her holy hell. I got to get back out front. Later."

Shanice didn't want to think about Cynthia. Nibbling at the edge of her consciousness was Gina's question. How did the reporter track Lisa back to Renee? How was she able to get Lisa's number from that one visit?

"No," she rebuked herself aloud. "This isn't my problem."

After a cup of tea and a plate of chocolate chip cookies, Shanice settled back at the desk to watch the clips she had assembled so far.

Dora Sampson's fingers played with the purple tips of her locs as she introduced herself. Then, they groped around until they found the fringe of her blouse. "I used to come to church nearly every day. I'd help Ms. Marietta in the soup kitchen on Tuesday, go to prayer service Wednesday, help Deaconess Cheryl with the clothing swap on Thursday, choir rehearsals... Anytime the doors were open, I was here. Ms. Barbara convinced me to get a life outside of church. 'Go to the movies,' she said, 'go dancing.' So I started volunteering other places. I even met a guy that I liked."

Gerald Lipscomb told a great story, but Shanice didn't really think the treasurer of the senior usher board understood his recording could be public. He was bald except for the wiry gray hair on his temples that appeared to hold his glasses in place. "Barbara Robinson and I disagreed a lot," he admitted freely. "We interpreted key scriptures differently and – frankly – she was wrong." Then, the boisterous zeal left his voice. "A time or two, I came to a meeting with a little taste on my breath. Maybe more than a little. She would always slide me a piece of chewing gum or mints without letting the others see. I appreciated that." Shanice made a note that his memory would be for the private family DVD only.

The thin man with creased, leathery skin introduced himself as Clarence Dearson. Wading through his tale of addiction for a sound bite hadn't been easy. "When Ms. Barbara talked with you, she could help you get to the root of the problem. She focused on what you really needed." A storm of emotion welled up in his chest, but he continued. "The world give up on you, family turn their back on you, *you* give up on you – not her. She knew how to get you reconnected with life again."

A middle-aged woman with her hands folded neatly in her lap sat poised and ready. Tailored burgundy jacket and easy smile, she looked like she could walk into any situation and feel comfortable. Unfortunately, she was also long-winded. "I'm Gloria Davis, founder and CEO of Whole Heart Collective, a program for young unwed mothers. When I started WHC a decade ago, I quickly ran into a roadblock. My girls didn't have any self-esteem. They covered it up with a lot of attitude and brusque language, but they were like little crushed flowers on the inside. You can't convince a girl to take care of her unborn child if she doesn't think she's worthy of love and care herself.

"Then Barbara Robinson came in during our first Christmas celebration to give them a pep talk. She reminded them that, as a known virgin, Mary's virtue was compromised when she turned up pregnant. We had forgotten that when Joseph found out about Mary's pregnancy, he was going to quietly break their engagement.

"Ms. Barbara reminded my girls that what other people see isn't what God sees. She told them that they were worth far more than they've been led to believe and encouraged them to find strength in their faith and in each other. It's been part of the curriculum ever since." She ended her talk with a definitive nod.

Shanice felt better. She hadn't done such a bad job on those. Committed to working on it for at least another hour, she chose another block of raw footage to watch.

"This is going to be on the website?" asked a young man in a glittering lavender blazer. Holding up a small compact, he combed his bangs. "I got a story, but I don't know if you'll be able to use it."

Unseen, Debra urged him to continue. "You're Robert, right? Say what you want; we'll find something we can use."

Robert nodded, sat back, and crossed his legs. "We've got a little conservative clique here who's always picking on somebody. Well, someone saw Gwen, a Sunday school teacher, out at the club and word got back to these folks. They cornered her after service to tell her it didn't look good for a servant of God to do unholy dances. Gwen told them to mind their business.

"Girl, they got hot! One of them ran and got Pastor Robinson and Ms. Barbara. Pastor tries to placate everybody; he agreed with Gwen but admonished her for being so tart tongued. But that wasn't enough for the clique. They started questioning if Gwen should even be teaching.

"Ms. Barbara shut it all down. She said if sinning on Saturday disqualified people from doing the Lord's work on Sunday, there would be nobody in the deacon row, on the choir or in the pulpit. She said we'd all be sitting in the pews waiting for angels to come down and start service.

"No one challenged her, not even Pastor." Robert clapped after each word to underscore his point. "She-had-them-shook!" He put a hand to his lips. "I need to stop before all the tea comes out."

The next interviewee was a stocky man who stood behind the chair. "The lighting down here isn't good at all." He turned his back to the camera and put both hands on his hips and inspected the tiny room. "You should be doing this in the balcony with the stained glass as a back drop."

"This is the space that was given to us, Deacon Louden." Shanice recognized the light, passive tone Debra used to soothe difficult customers.

Unfortunately, it did not work. "It's Elder Louden. Are we paying you for this? I don't recall approving any outside vendors in our last financial meeting."

"I don't know anything about that, sir."

"Since you are on our dime, you need to document the Keep Us Safe town hall meeting Saturday night. The mayor and Councilman Carter are supposed to be here – that's the kind of thing that should be on the website. You will be there?" It was more command than question.

"Sure," Debra said.

Shanice winced. Another promise made; she needed to

put a stop to this.

Elder Louden was not satisfied. "Humph. A new website was probably Barbara's idea. She was too independent for my tastes."

"Is that the memory you want to share, Elder Louden?"

"Of course not!" He sat down abruptly.

Chapter 32

Another nine-hour day under her belt, Debra washed her hands and forearms. The caffeine jolt from her lunchtime latte was wearing off. Helping out at the funeral had left her drained. She overheard her crew speculating about a wild night. They would never believe she was at church. Stepping into the sun felt good. Partially rejuvenated, she started out for home.

"Excuse me, miss?" At first, Debra didn't realize the wiry white guy waving a brochure was actually talking to her. His tone indicated that he didn't like having to work for her attention. "I have a question."

Johns Hopkins University shirt, black hair, face scarred from acne – this was the jerk who found sexually suggestive ways to ask Allison for samples. By the time he was ready to taste his sixth cheese, Debra put the grossed-out teenager on break and sent Theo to take over. The sample king immediately left without ordering anything. That was at least two hours ago.

"Yes," Debra said without breaking her stride. If he wanted answers, he'd have to keep up.

"My name is Brian." He put out his hand, but she looked around him to assess oncoming traffic. "I want more information about this Art of the Sandwich workshop. A three-hour course about throwing something between two slices of bread seems stupid to me."

Trained to give the workshop, Debra easily launched into a version of her welcoming narrative. "Fine ingredients, the proper blending of flavors, texture, and presentation –

all crafted with care – can transform any sandwich into a masterpiece."

"That's impressive. What if I don't want to take the class – does Chopin offer personal catering services?"

Debra caught a side glimpse of the leer spreading across his pocked cheeks. She continued to play clueless but decided to add an additional stop on her route. "For one sandwich, you can visit the Chopin Dining cascade. If you tell them what you are looking for, our master food preparers can whip up anything."

"I was thinking about a more personal, in-home touch. I bet you'd know how to handle my meat." Pleased with himself, Brian did not anticipate her ready response.

"Yes," Debra agreed, "I do know how to make a clean cut." She made a chopping motion with her hand that concluded in front of his groin.

She turned the corner and was in front of Clara's Rainbow Lounge. The women congregated in the smoking area outside of the bar spoke to Debra as she threaded through them towards the entrance. Their eyes were less welcoming when they fell on Brian and he stopped.

Debra smiled as if he were her favorite customer. "Good bye, Brian. And thank you for shopping at the Chopin Cart."

Happy hour at Clara's Rainbow Lounge included cheap well drinks and half-price bar snacks. Invited to join a table of acquaintances, Debra sank down in a worn leather chair to decompress. Her story riled up the others.

Cradling her rum and coke, Vanessa leaned back in her seat. "Deb, you should have cussed his perverted ass out when he was bothering that girl at the counter."

"Couldn't. I'd be written up." Debra moved her beer to make room for the newly arrived plate of nachos. Then she cleared her throat, sat up straight, and mimicked her boss' New England accent. "Chopin management would concede it was an immature prank but foul language toward a customer is never justified." She laughed and relaxed her shoulders.

"But that's sexual harassment."

"Short of a customer physically assaulting us or making other customers feel uncomfortable, we're strongly encouraged to take it all in stride. You can always take a five-minute yoga break to let the negativity energy flow out of you."

Vanessa and the other women were disgusted.

India leaned over the table to grab her share of chips. "Of course, a capitalist corporation is more concerned with the economic bottom line than with the safety of its employees."

Debra tried to stave off a diatribe against the patriarchal capitalistic power structure. "Listen, comrade. I called store security and told them what happened. They are making sure Allison gets home safely and keeping an eye out for Brian in general. Dude overplayed his hand when he approached me outside of the store."

Vanessa shushed the table. "Listen, stalkers are no joke. When my brother Ken worked in the mailroom for an accounting firm, he bragged about having a woman on every floor. None of them knew about each other. Five minutes here and there in a broom closet and they were buying him gifts. At the company Christmas party, one of his girlfriends sees him walking towards her group and says, 'Ruh-Roh, here comes trouble.' He'd paid her a visit that morning and she knew he was wearing his Scooby Doo drawers."

Debra laughed. "Are you serious?"

"He collects cartoon boxers. Anyway, it would have been a private joke between the two of them if other women in the room hadn't also seen him in his underwear. Ken was nervous for a few days, but no one went off on him. The women kept flirting and he kept delivering his package." Vanessa rolled her eyes. "Then, people started to complain about not getting mail in a timely fashion. Someone found a stack of mail from his route hidden in an empty cubicle. He started getting reprimands. Once his job was in jeopardy, his tires got slashed."

Latanya whistled sharply. "Somebody went after your boy's wallet."

Vanessa agreed. "Ken quit before they could fire him. The women never treated him differently to his face. He had no idea if it was one of them, all three of them, or someone else entirely. He hasn't had any problem since he left."

"I've got a story," Latanya said. She unbuttoned the top three buttons of her carrier uniform and fanned herself with a menu. "Erica, my straight buddy from work, was being stalked. A bunch of us would hang out from time to time. Erica would go home to all kinds of nasty voice mail messages or a phone ringing off the hook. This woman would call her a slut, a home wrecker, etc. Police didn't care and changing her number didn't help."

"They never care," India cut in. "They don't get paid to stop a crime; they show up after the fact."

Latanya gave her a fake smile before continuing. "Erica was a wreck. I gave her a ride home one day and decided to go inside with her. Like clockwork, the phone starts ringing. I answered it, prepared to give the creep every piece of my mind. Immediately, I recognized the voice." She paused and briefly made eye contact with everyone in her audience. "It was my girlfriend."

"Damn!"

"Whoa!"

"The woman had never said an insecure word to me," Latanya said, "but she was calling my friends – Erica wasn't the only one – to scare them. I confronted her and she cried about being afraid of losing me. It was a damned mess. I cut that psychopath loose quick."

Debra tapped Latanya on the arm. "How did she take the breakup? Did she leave you alone?"

"She'll walk right by me as if I'm not there, which is fine by me. I don't really think she's dangerous, but I'm not sure what Brandy would have done if I hadn't caught her."

Chapter 33

When Debra called asking for a ride home, Shanice didn't expect they would be making a stop at Brandeis Motors.

"Whatever you overheard at the bar doesn't matter. Cynthia already admitted to leaving the note."

"I didn't overhear anything. I got it directly from Brandy's ex-girlfriend." Debra crammed another piece of gum in her mouth. "Plus, you and Lisa have Renee in common; it's a solid theory."

"And Barbara was connected to her too." Shanice sighed and rested her forehead against the steering wheel. "It's going to bother me until I know for sure. Come on; let's get this over with."

The reception area contained a counter, a rack of air fresheners, and four plastic chairs for those who dared wait. A framed photograph of the Brandeis family was the centerpiece of a wall full of awards and commendations.

Though he was on the phone, the young man in attendance smiled at them when they walked in the door. He hung up and scribbled a few words on a note pad before inviting them forward. "Good evening, ladies. My name is Mike. It's too late to have anyone look at your car tonight. We could fit you in at 10:30 tomorrow."

"We don't need service," Shanice said. "I'd like to have a quick word with Brandy. Is she in?"

He opened the door behind him and looked into the garage. "I don't see her in the office. Probably doing a test drive. She should be back in a few minutes."

As they sat down, Shanice decided to limit their wait time to five minutes. Any longer than that would feel foolish. Debra sorted through the text messages buzzing for her attention while she leafed through a brochure about Brandeis Family Motors.

Harriet "Brandy" Brandeis was the youngest of five, the only girl and determined to follow in her father's footsteps. Though forbidden to get near the vehicles, she always managed to find her way under a hood. Proud of her stubborn determination, Duke Brandeis passed the business to her after he retired.

Between working at the garage, volunteering, and keeping up with Renee, did Brandy have time to stalk people?

Before Shanice could mention her doubts to Debra again, Brandy walked in from the garage. Smiling broadly, she handed a set of keys to Mike. "Call Mrs. Styles and let her know the Eldorado is ready. Put it on the invoice, but don't mention that we're giving her the senior discount. She thinks no one knows she's seventy-three."

Brandy froze briefly when she realized they had company. "Ladies, we don't take drop-ins and our calendar is full for the next two months. You'll have to take that silver eyesore somewhere else." Mike looked confused, but he had better sense than to contradict his boss.

The insult pissed Shanice off. "If you can't see us, I can take the issue somewhere else. I think we passed a police station on the way here."

Brandy's condescending smile vanished. "Follow me."

Inside the office, Brandy closed the door behind them and drew the curtains on the window that looked out on the garage floor. Debra immediately got comfortable. "You can't keep a woman unless you run everyone else away from her?"

Brandy got a cup of water from the dispenser in the corner, sat behind the desk, and shuffled some papers around. She spoke without making eye contact, her voice disinterested. "Relationship vultures see a mature woman dating someone younger and think it's open season. I let people know when they need to back off."

"Why don't you tell Renee to back off?" Shanice asked, her voice brimming with anger. She didn't want to be emotional, but she couldn't tamp down her anger. "She sent you away and you backed right on out with your tail between your legs. You didn't say anything to me either. When I left, you just watched me get in my car. Had to follow me around for a bit before you got up the nerve to leave a dirty message. That's pathetic."

Brandy scoffed. "I saw your car parked on the street and decided to leave you a little present. Nobody's stalking you. You're not worth the time."

The burning started in the pit of Shanice's stomach and spread up to her chest. If Debra hadn't been there, she would have bragged about going to Renee's studio and having lunch with her. She wanted to rub Brandy's nose in it. Taking a deep breath, she cooled the flames and continued. "Was Lisa spending too much time with Renee outside of the studio? Or do you call her students up at random?"

The papers stopped moving and Brandy looked up. This was worth her attention. "I didn't do anything illegal," she insisted. "I never threaten bodily harm or anything like that. If she took it as a threat, it had to be her conscience bothering her."

"I guess you didn't like Renee's friendship with Barbara Robinson either?"

"Hold on," Brandy sputtered. "I liked Ms. Barbara. She tried to convince Renee to settle down. When Ms. Barbara started telling her things she didn't want to hear, Renee cut her off just like that." She snapped her fingers.

Debra leaned forward, but Shanice touched her arm. Tears welled up in Brandy's eyes; the façade was cracking. After a tense moment of silence, she cried freely. "Renee is already through with me. She's got what she wanted and moved on. I helped her set that business up. I walked her through the legal paperwork, leasing the studio and figuring out a marketing plan. Now we barely talk."

Brandy dried her face with a handkerchief. "I went overboard; I'm sorry. She was grooming Lisa, someone she could be seen out in public with. That's why I ran her off. It was all for nothing. Now Renee's about to go on tour. From city to city, from bed to bed."

Shanice began tapping her leg. "Renee's not like that."

Brandy's bitter laughter caught them by surprise. "You don't know her. She initially told me you were some web designer who had a crush on her. I'm sure she's telling her prospective lovers that I'm just a friend who gave her some business advice." She licked her lips. "I could knock Renee right off that pedestal, destroy her wholesome image, but I don't like putting my business on front street."

"I don't get it," Debra said. "If Renee is so terrible, why do you still want her?"

Brandy shrugged and stared into her paper cup. "I'd still give Renee everything, but I don't have anything she wants."

Chapter 34

Gina laughed as she cooked dinner. Grandma Wilma would be scandalized to see her pouring jarred tomato sauce over browned ground beef. She dressed it up with fresh herbs, onions, and green peppers, but nothing she added could absolve her from the culinary sin. She gave everything a good stir before turning the flame down to a simmer.

Her mother and aunt had been dropping hints that they wanted to move one of the holiday meals to Gina's house, but she had been resistant. She'd always used the basement renovations as a reason to put them off. Truth was, she didn't want to deal with the draining, negative energy their family get-togethers brought with them. Grandma Wilma mocked Aunt Gloria's cooking nonstop last Thanksgiving, even as she reached for second helpings.

Gina decided to hold them off until next summer; she could host a 4th of July barbecue. That way, Uncle Kevin and Cousin Ryan could argue over the grill while everyone else looked for ways to keep cool.

She put bowtie pasta in a pot of boiling water and was pouring herself a glass of iced tea when the doorbell rang. She was surprised to find Officer Childress on the porch. "Hey. Is it okay if I take some measurements of the bar? I need to get a better idea of how much tile I should buy."

"I thought you weren't going to pick up more supplies until tomorrow." Gina anchored herself in the doorframe. She wasn't a fan of anyone, even friends, dropping by unannounced.

"The textile shop is closer to my place. I figure I should

174

stop by now instead of coming here in the morning and driving back to the store." Childress sniffed the air. "Either you dabbed some garlic behind your ears or you're cooking something good. Smells delicious."

"That was so corny. Come on in but no eating until Shanice and Debra get home."

"I don't want to disturb your evening, but if I do it now, it will save time tomorrow."

"Sorry for the attitude. I'm tired. The work that you're doing downstairs is fantastic. I couldn't see past the rotting shelves and worn out paneling, but you knew it could be so much more. Thank you."

"We've still got a little way to go. I'm going to throw some ambient lighting into the mix. The whole room should have an intimate glow."

"By the time you're through, I'll be able to charge admission."

"As long as I can get in for free."

"Of course."

As Childress went into the basement, Gina went back into the kitchen to make sure there were enough clean dishes for a fourth setting. She wondered what a date with her part-time carpenter would be like now. Could she break through the hard-shell of Childress and find Juanita again? Sighing, she decided to treasure their current relationship rather than long for the friend who had disappeared into her profession.

Childress returned carrying a calculator. "A little math and we're all set." She tried but failed to suppress a yawn.

"Catch a lot of bad guys today?" Gina pointed to a chair and then poured out a glass of iced tea for her friend.

Childress took a slow sip. "I got called out to Birket Court for a woman who locked her keys in her car. It was a bright, shiny white Mercedes purring like a kitten on a street full of garbage and tumble weave. The driver in distress was Molly from Ravenstone County."

"A white lady, in a white car, in a dark side of town,"

Gina said. "She was a long way from home."

"Yeah, it was suspicious to me too, so I called the plate in to make sure there was no funny business and it came back clean."

"Why did she get out of the car?"

"Molly is a good young lady who makes bad decisions. Her boyfriend Paul asked her to drive him down to the Birks. When they got there, he says he'll be back in a few minutes and disappears into an apparently abandoned building. Thirty minutes, no Paul. Meanwhile, the car grabs the attention of everyone who passes by. She gets out the car intending to knock on the door and get her man."

"It's a bad neighborhood, so she makes sure to lock the car door...with her keys inside."

"Bingo!" Childress said. "Several men hanging around offered to help, but they scared her. She thought I'd magically get the door open. Had to disappoint her; I'm not touching a Mercedes. Best I could do was babysit her until a tow truck came. Paul finally shows up. He's got ten years on her and smells like sour milk. The kind of guy that's nasty because he couldn't bother to change his underwear for the last week."

Gina crinkled up her nose. "I didn't need that visual."

"At least you didn't experience it live. He was not happy to see me. Suddenly, my radio goes crazy and two more squad cars appear. While I'm down there trying to sort it out, Mr. Paul Harrison, Sr. notices his favorite Mercedes is missing and files a report."

"You caught car thieves?"

"Yes and no. Mr. Harrison wanted the thieves to feel the full wrath of justice – until he realized the culprit was his son. It was a mess. Junior will probably get another round of community service." Childress stifled a yawn. "Did you go to Barbara Robinson's funeral?"

"Yeah. It was horrible and wonderful at the same time. I saw a lot of people that I grew up with, but being brought together for such a terrible reason... As my mother said,

Pastor Robinson put her away nicely."

"I heard it was packed to the rafters."

"Pretty much. Even the gossip columnist showed up."

"Cynthia?"

Gina smirked. "She didn't approach me, but she tried to convince Debra and Shanice to give her some dirt on Pastor Robinson. That was a bad idea; you can't tell your business in Hope Reborn without somebody hearing it."

"Gina?" Debra's voice rang through the house.

"In here!" Gina got up to check on the meal.

"Today was wild! Shanice and I –" Debra stopped abruptly when she saw Childress. "Hey. I didn't know we were having company tonight."

The police officer nodded back. "Hey."

"Dinner will be ready in a minute," Gina said. She turned around and Debra was gone. "Let me get them before they start playing video games."

"I got it," Childress said. She finished the last of her iced tea and smiled slyly. "Can you make me a plate to go?" Gina laughed and took the silverware out of the dishwasher.

Childress walked into the living room in time to see Shanice locking the front door. "Can I talk to you for a minute?"

Shanice reluctantly sat on the edge of the sofa. She had a lot to think about already. "What's up?"

"I told you to call me if Cynthia bothered you again."

"Haven't talked to her since Gina threw her out."

"Did you see her today?"

"No."

"Are you sure?"

Shanice sucked her teeth. "Why are you questioning me? Whatever Cynthia told you, it's a lie."

"Cynthia isn't saying anything. She's on life support."

"What happened?"

"She got hit by a car."

"Accident?"

"No, it hit her on purpose. She wasn't paying attention,

but witnesses say there was plenty of time for the car to avoid her. What we know for sure is that it was a gray car and a black woman was driving." Officer Childress had closed the distance between them and looked hard into Shanice's eyes. "Did you do it?"

Shanice was livid. "Are you seriously standing in my living room accusing me of running her down? My car is silver and almost collapses every time it hits a pothole."

"Maybe you didn't use your car."

"Childress, do you really think I would try to kill somebody?"

The officer grunted. "Don't give me that; you lied to me. I know you talked to Cynthia at the funeral. Maybe she got you alone and threatened you again."

"I saw her at the funeral, but she hasn't actually said a word to me since she left this house."

"This is my fault," Gina said, walking into the room. "Let me clarify. Shanice and Sarah, our church secretary, were by the baptismal pool when they overheard Cynthia trying to recruit Debra in the next room. That's what Sarah told me and everyone else who would listen." She got in the cop's face. "Now you answer a question for me. Why are you using our casual conversation to interrogate Shanice?"

Childress' eyes began to soften. "I wanted to make sure none of you were involved. If the hit and run can be traced back to the dinner party, I'll get in trouble for not reporting Cynthia and her boyfriend to Gerard."

"You didn't come here to get measurements at all, did you?" Gina ignored more explanations and opened the door. "You lied to your friends to get information to protect yourself. You've got your answers. You're safe. Go home."

"It wasn't like that!"

"There's nothing else here for you right now. I'll manage finishing the basement."

Head bowed to hide tears, Childress mouthed "sorry" to Shanice and walked into the night.

Full, Debra sat back and cast a mischievous look at Gina. "The women of Hope Reborn don't play. Which church mother tried to run her down?"

"You can't pin this on us." Gina poked at her with a fork. "Cynthia targeted half the congregations in the city. My cousin hasn't seen the inside of a church in a decade and she called to warn me about Ceeda Truth. The whole city hates her."

Unable to do more than pick at the food, Shanice pushed her plate aside and pulled out her phone. "You manipulate people, you make enemies. She should have expected someone to strike back eventually."

Gina raised a skeptical brow. "Talk like that will make you a prime suspect again."

"According to the news, it was a standard hit and run. The car didn't run over her, but she bounced off the bumper. She's in stable condition and being held in the hospital overnight for observation."

Debra chuckled. "Childress jumped the gun."

"She's not the only one," Shanice said. "You promised Elder Louden that we'd be there tomorrow to film that town hall."

"Right…sorry about that. I didn't really mean to commit you to it; I was trying to get him to sit down."

"I'm two-thirds through the videos. Are there going to be any more surprises?"

Debra scraped her plate and put it in the dishwasher. "Maybe. Just remember I was doing you a favor. I'm getting out of here before I get in more trouble." She stuck her tongue out at them before going upstairs.

Shanice's phone began vibrating. She rolled her eyes at the text.

"What's wrong?" Gina asked.

"Renee wants me to come over to her studio at 10am tomorrow so she can talk about Barbara. I got involved in all of this to help her out, not jump every time she snaps her fingers. That's a pattern I don't want to fall back into."

"Cut her some slack. With everything happening, she probably didn't have a chance to record her memory. You could make her write the reflection down instead."

"Nah, it will be easier to get it over with." Shanice took a sip of her drink, a ginger ale gone flat. "Besides, there are a few other things we need to talk about before I can move on."

It's about time, Gina thought as she smiled to herself.

Chapter 35

Shanice smiled as she got out of the car. After recording the reflection, she would lay out the truth about Brandy and watch Renee react in denial and anger. No matter the response, the spoiled princess would have to sort out her own mess. Since the affair with Brandy was winding down, there had to be at least one or two women waiting in the wings.

Renee would not be in control – a rare occurrence.

After loitering in the lobby for a few minutes, Shanice knocked on the studio door at exactly the appointed hour.

The smile Renee greeted her with quickly disappeared. She sighed. "You didn't even look at your phone, did you? I asked you to bring me a latte."

"Hi to you too," Shanice responded. She pulled the phone from her back pocket and saw notification for two missed text messages. "You could have called."

"It would have been rude to make a call in the middle of a lesson. Some of us do work during the day."

Shanice took a deep breath. "Let's not do this today."

Renee waved a hand in the air, signaling a truce. "All I'm saying is that you need to pay closer attention to what's going on around you." She noticed Shanice staring at her thighs and clapped her hands. "Hello, up here."

"Jeans and a sweater?"

"What's wrong with them?"

"I expected you to wear something holier for the church video."

"What are you talking about?"

181

"You said you wanted to see me about Barbara; I'm here to record your memory."

"No. I did that at church. " Renee balanced herself on a stool. "Brandy told me what she did."

Shanice felt the energy drain from her body. "What?"

Renee twisted her mouth and stared at the floor. "She came over last night after you confronted her. She confessed everything – what she did to you, Lisa, and others... I was so angry, but Brandy asked me to forgive her." She looked up. "We're going to try to work it out."

It took a moment for a bewildered Shanice to find her tongue. "What is there to work out? Brandy tried to scare everyone out of your life. That's textbook abuse."

"Brandy targeted younger women that she thought were interested in me. Barbara doesn't fit into that category, so I know Brandy didn't have anything to do with harassing her. That's what I wanted to talk you about. I don't want you going around insinuating that she had anything to do with Barbara's death."

"You don't know that. Why would you protect her?"

"I don't want you to be as reckless as when you thought it was that gossip columnist. Plus, I don't need any rumors in the air to discourage potential clients. Just forget it ever happened, okay?"

"Does Brandy have something on you?"

"Excuse me?"

Shanice tried to piece together a scenario that made sense. "Cynthia is in the hospital. Did you try to run her over? Did Brandy let you borrow a car from her lot?"

"You're quick with an accusation. I can play that game too." Renee put her hands in her lap and struck her innocent, wide-eyed pose. "Maybe you're an obsessive ex-girlfriend. Barbara threatened to out me and she's killed. Did you get rid of her? Did Brandy save her own life by coming clean before you could warn me about her?"

Shanice backed into the wall. Her eyes, her flesh, everything was on fire. Her actions – distorted and twisted

– could fit any frame. "Stop, please stop. Maybe I was stupid for trying to look out for you. I wouldn't hurt anyone."

"I know. Me, you, Brandy – none of us had anything to do with Barbara's murder. Let it go."

Shanice waned to bolt, but she couldn't leave without asking one final question. "Is being with Brandy better than being with--" Fear seized her tongue at the last second. "Better than being single?"

Renee considered her answer carefully. "Shanice, we broke up because you wanted more than I can give. Brandy doesn't want more; she's trying to save what we have. There's a difference."

Shanice fast-forwarded through the last hour of raw footage to find Renee's message. The singer sat down, confused. "I thought Shanice was recording the videos?"

"I'm the second string," Debra said off screen.

"I didn't know she was hiring staff now. It's good to see the business growing."

"You and Shanice are friends?"

"I'm a former client." Renee reapplied her lipstick and checked her eyeliner. "Sorry, I need another moment to get myself together." She closed her eyes and took several deep breaths. When she opened them, they brimmed with tears.

Dabbing at wet cheeks with a monogrammed handkerchief, the singer signaled she was ready to begin. "I met Barbara years ago when she was one of the judges at a local gospel competition. I competed as a soloist and you couldn't tell me I wasn't the best voice in the building. My performance was flawless; I had camera presence and everything. When I didn't win, I approached accused the judges of playing favorites. Honestly, I was an egotistical little brat."

"You still are," Shanice whispered.

Renee produced a sad smile for the camera. "Barbara took the time to give me feedback. She explained that even though my singing was fine, it didn't feed the crowd spiritually. She challenged me to go beyond memorizing notes and words, to bridge the connection between the lyrics and my own personal testimony. She helped me understand that singing was a real ministry and the first person you minister to is yourself. It's a lesson I try to teach my own students. I'm going to miss her."

Renee held the sorrowful expression for two beats. "How was that?"

"Perfect."

"Tell Shanice I want a copy of this for my website."

Shanice watched it twice. Her anger gave way to a stunning realization. Renee manipulated with such ease that she never had to lie. She knew the women who wanted her would ignore what they didn't want to see.

It was not an unfamiliar technique. In college, Shanice had made a practice of telling women she wasn't interested in relationships. That didn't stop her from accepting girlfriend-level gifts from Laura or going along when Andie invited her on family trips. When they got upset, she chastised them for not believing her anti-relationship stance.

With Renee, she had fallen into the same trap. That was why the break-up hurt so much.

Feeling tired and empty, Shanice went out on the back porch. Waning sunrays and the scent of barbecue traveling on the wind were a welcome distraction.

Gina joined her. "How did it go?"

"Brandy has a reputation for mistreating women. I thought Renee should know."

"She didn't believe you?"

"Didn't get a chance to tell her. Brandy came clean and told her everything last night."

"That was smart," Gina said. "A good business woman knows the art of damage control."

"They cried about it. They're going to try to work it out."

"It can be easy to mistake drama for love."

Shanice's right foot was restless. "Got that closure I was

looking for. Turns out we're not compatible."

"Excuse me? That's no secret. I told you that."

"Yeah, I know." Shanice groaned. "Everybody told me."

Gina's phone beeped, prompting her to frown. "Childress needs to stop wearing down my battery."

"It could have been worse. She could have taken me downtown for questioning or delivered me to Detective Gerard."

"You can forgive her if you want to," Gina said. I'll have to think about it."

"Don't be petty." Shanice couldn't believe it when the words tumbled out of her own mouth. "Brandy isn't the only person who should get a second chance."

Chapter 36

After breakfast, Debra and Shanice transformed the dining room table into an editing bay. With hours of raw footage left to process, Shanice made a tough decision. "Let's concentrate on making a DVD for the family. That's where the full stories will go. Not everyone will make it to the web memorial and those that do won't have more than one line."

Debra shrugged. Her second cup of coffee had kicked in and she was ready to take on any challenge. "I can trim the parts where people introduce themselves and put in a text overlay with the name. I have this really nice stained-glass font."

"That sounds time consuming."

"Not really. Besides, I'm sure the family won't recognize everyone otherwise. Look, I've already done a few."

College senior Kara Banks tearfully recalled how Ms. Barbara was the only one who supported her decision to go to school out of state. "It made my mother mad, but I needed to be away from home to come into my own. Mom wanted Ms. Barbara to remind me that disobeying parents was a sin, but Ms. Barbara reminded her that parents shouldn't vex their children."

Deaconess Martha Jackson wore a wide-brimmed hat that encased her face in shadow. "I went to altar call once and asked for a prayer for my grand baby," she spoke in a delicate but purposeful tone. "I was having a hard time keeping him away from bad influences. Mrs. Robinson contacted me a few days after service and got him into a football camp. I didn't have to worry about him during the day and he was too tired to run the streets at night."

As each woman spoke, her name faded in at the bottom of the screen and sparkled before fading out.

"Those look great," Shanice admitted. "It's not going to be what the job is worth, but I'd like to pay you something for your time."

"No, let me do this. Between Cynthia and Elder Louden, I owe you."

Shanice winced. "Do you know he called this morning? The town hall meeting is now a whole day community event. He left a detailed explanation of the schedule and his expectations of my staff."

"Staff?"

"You, of course. He said you are rude and needed training." Shanice drummed her fingers against the table. "I wasn't hired to become the church archivist; he's not even the person in charge of this project. I don't want to deal with any of this stuff right now."

Debra queued up another raw clip. "Why don't you take the morning off? Go out for a while; just bring me back something decent for lunch."

"Thanks. I don't want to be staring at a screen all day. Maybe I'll go to the movies or something."

Debra tried sucking in her lower lip until the moment passed, but the temptation was too great. "Hard to avoid screens, big ones, at the movie theater." She yelped in mock pain when Shanice plucked her on the forehead.

Because she didn't have Sarah's phone number, Shanice found herself knocking on the side door of Hope Reborn. As an entrepreneur, she knew skipping out on a job could destroy her reputation. She needed to explain the miscommunication to Sarah, establish boundaries, and be on her way.

When the door opened, Shanice stepped into a whirl of activity. The open space had been divided into two sections.

Round tables in the front had full place settings in a white and purple theme. Local service organizations set up displays on rectangular tables in the back. The church office was locked.

Shanice approached a girl creating flower arrangements. "Excuse me, I'm looking for Sarah."

The teenager looked up briefly as she tied purple roses with white ribbon. "She went to the store. We're low on paper plates and cups. Elder Louden is coordinating the community volunteers. He's in the sanctuary."

Shanice stepped back. That was a man she wanted to avoid. "I'm not a volunteer. Is Pastor Robinson around?"

"He's next door. I can walk you over."

An older woman who had her back to them turned around. "Make sure you come right back, Tarsha. You have to help me put up the balloons."

Tarsha waited until they walked away before sucking her teeth.

A young man playing a game on his phone was spread across the steps of the annex house. He stood up as they drew near. Shanice recognized him as the college sophomore who had breezed through math classes in high school but could not easily master Statistics 101. Ms. Barbara convinced him there was no shame in needing help. With a tutor, he squeezed out a B-. "Sorry," he said. "Can't let you in."

Tarsha rolled her eyes. "Move, Jason."

"Nope." Jason folded his arms. "House isn't open. The last thing they want is some little kid running around inside."

Tarsha pointed to Shanice. "She needs to talk to Pastor Robinson. It's important."

The cocky gleam faded from his eyes. "Okay. She can get in, but you can't."

They were still arguing when Shanice closed the door behind her. The scent of pine soap hung heavily in the air. The entire house had been scrubbed down. Even though opened curtains welcomed sunshine, a spirit of sadness prevailed. The low wail of Mahalia Jackson came from above.

Following the music led Shanice to Ms. Barbara's classroom. The blood was gone and so was the desk. In its place was a table bearing a white candle and a bowl containing a bundle of smoking sage. "Precious Lord" streamed from a portable record player on the floor. In the corner of the room, a woman draped in white sat with her hands covering her heart. Eyes closed, her face tilted to the ceiling.

As Shanice edged forward, the floor beneath her creaked. The woman opened her eyes and beckoned her forward. "Don't be afraid; come in." Taking a remote from the folds of her dress, she turned down the music. "My name is Erin. Can I help you?"

Feeling queasy, Shanice had to remind herself to breathe. "I was looking for Pastor Robinson. I didn't mean to disturb you."

"He was here a few minutes ago; I'm not sure where he is now."

"What are you doing, if you don't mind me asking?"

"The mark a traumatic event leaves on a space is multi-layered. Both a physical and spiritual cleaning is required." Erin smiled. "I know it looks odd. When I approached Pastor about doing this, he agreed. He said Ms. Barbara wouldn't mind."

Shanice's gaze drifted to the place Ms. Barbara had fallen. "Doesn't matter how much you clean," she said, her voice cracking. "No one will be able to forget what happened."

Erin walked over to Shanice and held out her hand. "May I?"

"Um, okay." Shanice took the hand reluctantly.

Erin massaged her wrist. "Just breathe. Relax into the natural rhythm of your body."

Shanice felt a renewing sense of calm as tension left her body.

Erin smiled. "Spiritual cleansing is not about forgetting. It's about siting in this room without anger or anxiety." A loud thump from above startled them. "I think we've found Pastor."

Chapter 37

"Hello?" Shanice called as she made her way up to the third floor landing. Walking through an open door, she saw a woman sitting at a table and sorting through bags filled with clothes. "Hi. Is Pastor Robinson up here?"

The startled woman yelped, took a defensive stance and pulled her over-sized purse under the table. Then, her eyes softened. "Wait, you're Shanice. The new webmaster. We've run into each other a couple of times."

"Right. Deaconess Cheryl." As Shanice extended her hand, it was hard to reconcile the person wearing makeup and a red, open neck blouse with her memory of the homely woman she met in the past. When they crossed paths before, the deaconess' head had always been covered. The loose finger waves were a surprise. "I'm only designing the site. Sarah will be handling everything once it's set up."

"You can just call me Cheryl. Is there anything I can help you with?"

Ready to get far away from Hope Reborn, Shanice decided explaining the situation to the deaconess fulfilled her professional obligation. "Elder Louden wanted me to bring the crew back to document today, but that's outside of my contract with the church. As far as I know, he's not affiliated with the web project. I wanted to clear up any confusion in case Pastor Robinson was expecting me."

Cheryl raised her arched eyebrows. "Louden knows better than that. He likes to insert himself in business that is clearly not his. If Sarah's in charge, don't listen to anyone else. She doesn't work through third parties."

"Good. I didn't want to charge the church for a service your own media team can cover."

"Can you do me a favor? Help me take some bags over to the sanctuary?" Cheryl pointed to a cluster of bags in the corner. "I'm setting up the table for the clothing ministry."

"No problem." Shanice ventured into a barely lit section of the room. She wondered if the deaconess wanted a little companionship or a volunteer to do heavy lifting. After a few minutes, she would use her lunch date with Debra as an excuse to leave. "How did the town hall turn into an all-day affair?"

"Since Ms. Barbara's death, the mayor has a police car to sit outside of the church on weekends and increased foot patrols during the week. Pastor worries the special attention is driving a wedge between us and our neighbors. The fair is to reaffirm that we are part of this community."

Shanice panicked when a centipede slithered across the bag in her arms. She dropped the clothes and stumbled into a cluster of webs. Flailing her arms only made it worse.

"My goodness, are you okay?" Cheryl stifled her laugh with a men's dress shirt. Regaining her composure, she went back to folding shirts into neat squares. "I should have warned you, the janitor rarely makes it past the second floor. There's a bathroom behind you."

The bare overhead bulb cast the dank room in a weak yellow light. Shanice slapped at her neck; it felt like bugs had found a way under her t-shirt. She grabbed a handful of paper towels and soaked them in water.

Cheryl continued in the other room. "I want to thank you for not trying to gouge us. People always want something from the church – which is fine – but need can easily out-pace resources."

Shanice felt like she was rubbing grime deeper into her face. It took three wipe downs for the itching to stop. Tossing her refuse in the wastebasket, she noticed a rag smeared with dried makeup and other stains. She looked around the room. Thick layers of dust blanketed everything except the sink, a near empty bottle of soap, and the mirror.

Shrugging off her unease, Shanice picked up two bags.

"Take those over to Mother Banks," Cheryl said. "Tell her I want the clothes divided into three categories: casual wear, dressier outfits, and items suitable for job interviews. Hopefully, they won't end up in a big heap of confusion."

By the time Shanice reached the sidewalk, her arms were tired. The bags grew heavier with each step. She was happy to see Elder Louden on the sanctuary steps. He didn't offer to help with the burden, but he did hold the door open for her. "Bout time you got here," he said. "Are those donations?" Confused, he looked beyond her, "Is the rest of the crew already inside?"

Shanice didn't stop. "I'm leaving after I drop these off with the clothing ministry," she said over her shoulder. "My contract with the church doesn't include filming random events."

He followed her down the steps. "But I was told--"

"Mr. Louden," a teenage boy called from across the room. "Do you have the key to the craft closet? We need crayons for the coloring table."

Though glaring at her, Louden walked off toward a group of young children.

Mother Banks eagerly accepted the clothes but rolled her eyes as Shanice relayed the instructions. "Those categories don't work anymore. Girls wear pajama bottoms out in the street and jeans to work. We're grouping things by size." She turned to the young lady helping her. "Mya, see if you can get another table."

As Shanice watched the women set about their work, she realized the answer to an important question was right in front of her. No one saw a blood-drenched suspect fleeing the scene because the killer went to the third floor, cleaned up, and changed clothes.

She thought back to that horrific day. Police hadn't searched the third floor because the door was locked. They assumed the assailant was a random stranger, not someone who would have a key.

Shanice wasn't sure what to do. She wanted to call Detective Gerard or Childress, but she didn't have any evidence. They would probably ignore her. What if they did listen to her --and she was wrong? She didn't want to be responsible for an innocent person getting tangled up in a slow-moving justice system.

"Shanice?" Mother Banks waved a handkerchief at her. "Unless you're picking out something for a young one, can you step aside?"

Shanice moved out of the way of a pregnant woman trying to reach baby clothes. "Sorry about that."

"And don't get rooted in that spot either," Mother Banks said. "Plenty of work left; do something."

Shanice nodded and began walking. *I need to go back to the third floor.*

Chapter 38

"It's me again," Shanice said. "I wanted to let you know that I ran into Elder Louden. No need to pass on the message."

Cheryl stifled a laugh. "How did he take it?"

"Not well, but he didn't have time to argue." Shanice walked over to the table. "Mother Banks asked if there are more children's clothes."

"Hmm. That's going to be tricky." Cheryl looked around the room. "Try the bags under the window. The one on the right."

Loosening the drawstring revealed a tangle of brightly colored clothing. Shanice bent over to get a closer look. "That's amazing," she said. "All of these bags look the same to me – how can you tell what's in any of them?"

"Making order out of chaos is a gift. I don't have an elaborate system – just a good memory."

"I can't imagine Mother Banks getting up here, but the other members don't move things around?"

"Not without my supervision. I'm the only one with a key."

Shanice felt lightheaded and reached out to the wall to steady herself.

"Be careful," Cheryl said. "We're on a slight incline; it's easy to lose your balance."

"I'm okay." Standing straight, Shanice re-oriented herself. "You have a great memory. Did you record a remembrance for Ms. Barbara?"

Cheryl moved on to sorting the pants. She motioned for

Shanice to bring a bag to the table. "No, my husband did. Bernard has been a member here all his life and saw her as an auntie."

"I can't imagine the pain Pastor Robinson is going through. My longest relationship was two years. To be in a loving relationship for decades – that's almost a miracle."

"Well," Cheryl said. "He was devoted to her." Without looking up from her task, she added, "She left him once."

"Do you mean the time Ms. Barbara went to take care of her dying friend?"

"It was more than that. When Barbara Robinson went away, she took everything. Bernard and I stopped by to make sure Pastor was properly being taken care of. There wasn't any hint of a woman's touch in the place – not even in the bathroom. She was coming to church all pious while she had abandoned him." Cheryl teared up. "Pastor Robinson had to keep up the charade for the others, but I knew."

Looking out the window, Shanice saw Pastor Robinson talking with a group of neighbors in front of the church. "I've never been to a service, but I thought they had a reputation for avoiding extravagance."

Cheryl's laughter echoed through the room. "Barbara wore those ugly outfits at church, but she wasn't frugal at all. I saw her at La Petite Grange, that fancy restaurant at the Bitmore-Key Inn. Pastor was nowhere in sight and there she was ordering the most expensive things on the menu."

Shanice couldn't believe it. It hadn't occurred to them that the pictures intentionally focused on the food. There were no life-shattering, career-ending secrets on the verge of being divulged. A jealous parishioner wanted the pastor to know his wife had an expensive meal. "I guess everyone needs to splurge sometime." Then she remembered the pictures taken in the hotel room. Her amusement turned to disgust, but she didn't let it show. "Did you tell Pastor Robinson?"

"I showed him," Cheryl said, "but I knew there was

nothing he could do about her hypocrisy. She constantly undermined his authority, making him feel small. Everybody thought Barbara was so holy, but I saw her for what she really was."

As the deaconess continued to talk, Shanice decided to take a risk. "What happened when you confronted her?"

"That prune-faced witch acted like she didn't know what I was talking about. She told me not to bother her and went back to writing out the lesson." Cheryl clenched a pair of jeans to her chest. "She wrote 'Jezebel' on the chalkboard and started laughing."

And there it was. Shanice clasped her hands together to keep them from striking out. "Is that why you killed her? Because she laughed?"

Cheryl's whole body trembled, trying to throw off the accusation. "No, of course not. That happened weeks ago. I wasn't even at the church when she died."

"You murdered Ms. Barbara and came up here to change your clothes. You were actually leaving, not arriving, when Deaconess Odessa saw you in the car. If she'd come outside a minute sooner, she would have seen you coming out of the house."

"That's a lie. What's wrong with you? Why are you saying these things?"

Shanice took a step closer. "Ms. Barbara wouldn't have turned her back on a stranger; she turned her back on you. She was going to tell her husband that you sent those pictures. Angry, embarrassed, full of hate--you killed her." The denials stopped. Fear flooded Cheryl's eyes. "Pastor Robinson is going to be angry at himself for not seeing you for what you really are."

Cheryl grabbed Shanice's arm. "No, you don't understand. I freed him. He doesn't have to pretend anymore. I can take care of him."

"He didn't want you before and he's not going to want you now. You murdered his wife." Shanice twisted out of her grasp. "What about the husband you already have?

Jezebel!"

Arms swinging widely, Cheryl attacked.

After deflecting the blows, Shanice pushed the deaconess back hard. "It's a little different when you're not fighting an old woman."

Screaming, Cheryl ran down the steps. "Help," she yelled. "She's trying to kill me!"

Shanice retrieved the purse from under the table. It was heavier than she expected.

Once outside, Cheryl pushed through the crowd and flung herself at Pastor Robinson. Between sobs and gulps of air, she struggled to speak. "That woman attacked me." She pointed at Shanice, who was just coming out of the door.

Shanice propped open the purse to reveal a damaged bookend on top of a crumpled, bloody dress. "Call the police," she said quietly. "Cheryl killed Ms. Barbara."

Pastor Robinson stared down at the deaconess in disbelief. "Why? Why would you hurt my wife?"

Tears were gone, but the trembling voice remained. "No," Cheryl pleaded. "She's a liar. I could never do anything to hurt you. I love--"

"Cheryl!" Bernard Hoffman rushed out of the church towards them. "We've got to get to the lot. The police are there with a warrant." He noticed his wife's disheveled appearance and the tears streaming down Pastor Robinson's face. "What's going on?"

Shrinking back from the angry voices around her, Cheryl covered her face and collapsed into a heap on the sidewalk.

Chapter 39

A clean-shaven Detective Gerard greeted Shanice when she arrived at the police station to record her witness statement. He offered her coffee and didn't rush her through the interview. Though his questions were thorough, none of them veered toward Pastor Robinson's love life.

Shanice appreciated this gentle approach. All of her courage from yesterday was gone and she felt drained. The phone rang all night. Though the police had whisked her away before any press showed up, that hadn't stopped her name from appearing in the evening news. Many people had witnessed her accusing Cheryl of murder and they were more than happy to tell reporters what they saw.

When it was over, Gerard smiled and led her to his office. He took a breath before squeezing behind a desk that did not give him enough leg room. There was a spare suit hanging behind the door and an aqua-blue bottle of aftershave sat atop a file cabinet.

Shanice couldn't help but acknowledge his change in demeanor. "I had been dreading this all day. To be honest, I thought you were going to be upset with me."

Detective Gerard sighed. "It's a nuisance when civilians interfere with ongoing investigations. Television has every idiot convinced they are Poirot. However, if you hadn't acted, the suspect would have destroyed important evidence. I'm happy to make an exception in this case." He studied her silently for a moment. "How are you doing?"

"Okay. I need about eight hours of sleep and all of the

newscasters to forget my name."

"Now that Hoffman is in custody, all the formerly tight-lipped church folks want to help me." Detective Gerard batted his eyes quickly and spoke in an airy falsetto. "Cheryl never had anything nice to say about Ms. Barbara and she dressed her husband in clothes Pastor Robinson donated to the clothing ministry. I thought the young couple was struggling. I didn't realize she had a fetish."

Though she wanted to laugh, Shanice could only manage a weary chuckle. "It was obvious you were trying to point the finger at Pastor Robinson. They closed ranks to protect him."

"But my instinct was correct." He tapped his nose. "Cheryl Hoffman may have acted independent of the pastor, but my gut told me there was another woman."

"May have?"

Detective Gerard shrugged. "I always leave a little room for doubt; it's part of the job." He took a pamphlet from a desk drawer and stapled his business card to it. "Ms. Wilkins, you've been through a traumatic experience. Sleep may not be the only thing you need. We have a program for witnesses to help them process what they are going through. You have any trouble dealing with the aftermath, call these good folks here or call me."

"Thank you."

"I know your name is already out there, but the state will not publicly discuss your involvement in the case. If we need anything further, either myself or the district attorney will be in touch. We prefer that you don't discuss the case with outsiders. Understand?"

Shanice nodded. "Completely.

"Great. Do you need a ride home?"

"No, I drove."

Detective Gerard picked up the phone and dialed an extension. "Can you escort Ms. Wilkins to her vehicle? Thanks." He hung up. "We don't like civilians roaming around unaccompanied."

The office door opened and Childress popped her head in. "Ready to go?"

Shanice slung her backpack over her shoulder and followed Childress through a maze of cubicles. "So, is Detective Gerard always so relaxed in the office?"

"No, and it's not going to last long. That's a post-case glow. I think he gets to stand near the podium if there's a press conference about the arrest." Childress shifted her weight from foot to foot as they waited for an elevator. "Gina has finally started talking to me again and I understand you're responsible for that."

Shanice shrugged. "No hard feelings on my part. I know you were just doing your job."

"I should have been straightforward, treated you like a friend. I approached the situation assuming you would lie to me. That was a mistake and I'm sorry." Childress opened a side door for her that led directly to the parking lot.

"Apology accepted. Can you walk me all the way to the car?"

"Sure. What's up?"

When they were some distance from the building, Shanice whispered. "Did Cheryl confess?"

"I have no idea and, if I did, I couldn't tell you. Didn't Detective Gerard tell you this is a different level of the game? Any discussion could jeopardize the case and my job."

"Come on, tell me something. What's going to happen to her?"

"That's up to her lawyer and the DA. Now, if I had a client who was accused of murdering a cherished community leader, I'd want to take a plea bargain and settle it with as little fanfare as possible."

"Okay. On to a different subject. Are you ever going to ask Gina out?"

Officer Childress rolled her eyes and laughed. "Right now, I'm happy she's letting me finish the basement. Go home and stay out of trouble."

Chapter 40

Shanice dumped clean clothes from the laundry basket onto the couch. She searched frantically through the pile, but underwear eluded her. Gina observed the action from the recliner. "Fold the clothes. It will be easier to find whatever you're looking for."

The wall clock chimed the quarter hour and Shanice bristled. "I'm meeting Pastor Robinson in forty-five minutes. Do I have enough time to wash and dry a quick load?" Three weeks had passed since she left the heartbroken minister crying on the sidewalk. They had spoken on the phone, but she was nervous about seeing him again.

"You can always go as you are. Put on a full-length coat and no one will know you're in your pajamas."

Walking out of the kitchen, Debra stopped short when she discovered a pile of t-shirts in her usual spot. Shanice shooed her away. "Don't get my clothes dirty."

Debra leaned against the banister. "Guess who I saw yesterday?" She took a mouthful of oatmeal and waited, but neither roommate took up her challenge. "Ms. Cynthia Tavares."

"Here?" Shanice's heart raced at the thought of the gossip columnist coming back into their lives.

"At the Chopin Cart. Her leg is in a boot and she was using a cane. She hobbled away quick when she saw me behind the counter."

Stretching, Gina slipped on her shoes. "Since she's been exposed, the *Edmondson Enquirer* is running stories about

Cynthia. Trust me; she wants no parts of us. Oh, I meant to tell you – don't wait up for me tonight."

Shanice gave up on panties and plucked a pair of boxers from a mound of socks. "Gina, hot date tonight?" She winked at Debra.

"Surprise party for our office manager. Brazilian steakhouse with open bar." Gina patted her belly. "I figure if I go to the gym now, my body will forgive me later. Step it up; you only have twenty-five minutes."

Her eyes focused on the floral pattern on the teacup, Lisa pulled the delicate china towards her. She watched cream become billowy clouds in her Earl Grey. Her slender fingers fluttered over the sweeteners before picking two white packets.

Shanice and Pastor Robinson exchanged hesitant glances. They had invited Lisa to lunch at La Petite Grange to offer apologies and an explanation. Having ordered their entrees, it was time to push past awkward pleasantries.

Shanice had to advocate hard for this meeting. She thought Lisa deserved the truth or, at the very least, a version of it that would let her walk in the world at ease. From Pastor Robinson's perspective, the killer had confessed and Barbara's legacy was intact. Acknowledging any wrongdoing could foolishly put Hope Reborn in jeopardy. His initial response was a curt "No!"

The pastor called back a few days later and admitted that his reaction was rooted in selfishness. Lisa deserved to be released from the burden of fear.

Inviting Lisa to lunch involved asking her in person. Shanice decided a potential scuffle with ushers was better than popping up at the school again. Thankfully, her worst fears did not come to fruition. Lisa was grateful for the invitation; she wanted to understand what happened.

"I'm sorry I showed up at your school like that," Shanice began. "We assumed you were involved and didn't think about any negative impact our actions could have."

Lisa shifted in her seat. "I was so scared. What if you had killed Barbara? What if you had been stalking both of us?"

"Barbara and I were scared too," Pastor Robinson said. "We were guided by our worst fears and got it terribly wrong. Barbara knew the truth before she passed."

"They did arrest the killer, right? It's not another person of interest?"

Pastor Robinson nodded. "Cheryl Hoffman, a member of our congregation, confessed. Last year, we noticed Cheryl wearing a scarf Barbara had donated to the clothing ministry. Barbara took her aside and asked that she not build her wardrobe from items gifted to the church. Cheryl has been obsessed with finding fault in Barbara ever since. We never suspected it would lead to this."

The conversation stopped abruptly when the waiter returned with their appetizers. Shanice prodded her salad before taking over the story. "Cheryl overheard Barbara making plans for your girls' weekend. She decided to show up and get some pictures. For her, the lavish meal was the sin; it had nothing to do with you at all."

"What?" Lisa's face was a mixture of relief and confusion.

Pastor Robinson took a deep breath. "Cheryl thought she was exposing Barbara's secret extravagant lifestyle," he said. "She sent the pictures to me anonymously thinking I would publicly reprimand my wife. When that didn't happen, Cheryl took it upon herself to confront Barbara and lost control." He pushed his plate away and sucked in his bottom lip.

Lisa, fighting back her own tears, touched his shoulder. "I'm so sorry."

Shanice gave an abridged version of the aftermath. "She hit Ms. Barbara from behind with the closest object within reach, a statuette. She went to the third floor where clothing donations were kept, hid the statue, changed clothes, and cleaned herself up. When we were coming in the front door, she was slipping out the back. Then she pretended to arrive after the body was found."

Lisa sat quietly, turning the information over in her mind. "What about the phone calls?"

Shanice knew this moment would come. As hurt as she was about Brandy, she couldn't bring herself to betray Renee. "Different person, but Barbara was still the target. Ceeda Truth, the gossip columnist, targeted friends of the Robinsons. I don't know how she got your number, but she tricked her way into my house by befriending one of my roommates." She took a gulp of ginger ale to wash the lie out of her mouth.

"That's horrible. She can't get away with it, can she?"

Though back in control of his emotions, Pastor Robinson held on to his handkerchief. "Ceeda Truth is already reaping the evil she sowed. When Cheryl found out this woman was trying to hurt me, she ran the reporter down. Despite a forged temporary tag, they were able to trace the car back to Hoffman's Motors."

"I think the murder was starting to wear on Cheryl," Shanice offered. "She was eager to talk about her hatred of Ms. Barbara; the police would have drawn a confession out of her. My encounter with her just sped the process along."

Pastor Robinson reached into his breast pocket and took out a business card. "I can't envision Cheryl changing her plea, but it's possible that the press could find out about your lunch with Barbara. I know your school can be paranoid about appearances. If there's any trouble, I'd be happy to talk someone into seeing sense."

Lisa reluctantly took the card. "I'm leaving at the end of the semester. Can I use you as a reference?"

"Of course. Anything I can do to help, just ask."

Lisa stared down at the leaves in the bottom of her cup. "Barbara warned me that creating a secret life would hurt rather than protect me. She was right. I couldn't call the police to report the harassment. I couldn't go to her funeral." She looked up at them. "I don't want that life. I can't be afraid to live."

Chapter 41

After they watched Lisa leave, Shanice motioned for Pastor Robinson to join her on an ornate sofa in the Bitmore-Key lobby. "How are you doing?"

He sighed. "I've been waiting for things to go back to normal, but that's impossible. Even when Barbara lived with Dorothy, we talked every day." He paused to calm the storm welling in his eyes. "It's hard – especially having to put on a strong face in public."

"You don't have to be strong; people know you're grieving."

The corner of his lips twitched into a temporary smile. "Oliver makes the same argument. The truth is, you get to have one good cry. After that, leaders can't appear vulnerable."

"The press leaving you alone?"

The minister tugged at his jacket sleeve. "The double murder on Carston knocked us from the TV news. The paper is doing spin-off stories now, but those articles aren't on the front page. They've stopped calling me but are still reaching out to members of the congregation."

Shanice recalled seeing an article on the pressures of being a pastor featuring other religious leaders. Even Elder Louden had a chance to tell his story. "I know it's little consolation, but in everything I've read, Barbara is remembered fondly."

"What about you?"

"A few reporters reached out, but their interest in me petered out quickly. I explained that as a potential witness, the district attorney asked me not to speak about the case." They sat silently for a few minutes, reflecting on all that had happened.

Compassion kept Shanice from bringing up the inconsistencies in the story he told the police. She believed that Pastor Robinson had discovered his wife's bludgeoned body before she arrived. In a fit of panic, he assumed "Jezebel" was written by the killer and erased it. Then he went back to the office and waited to "find" the body.

Shanice knew there was no way to prove the scenario put forth by her imagination. The cold, ashy hands he greeted her with that morning didn't count as evidence. Still, it had to be eating him up inside to know that while he was washing the blackboard, Cheryl was above changing out of her bloody clothes.

Pastor Robinson cleared his throat. "Bernard is the one I'm worried about. Everything he's worked so hard for has been ripped away. I call to pray with him sometimes."

Shanice did a double take. "That's extremely generous. He had to know that his wife was obsessed with you. She dressed him in your old clothes."

"Men don't keep track of things like that. Your wife puts a tie on you, you don't second guess where it came from. Besides, I am still his minister. Bernard is trying to do right, but he's not sure what that is."

The grandfather clock chimed the hour. Shanice stood up. "I have a few more errands to run before I get back home," she said. "Thank you for coming out. I know that was difficult."

Pastor Robinson needed a little help getting to his feet. They shook hands. "When we're wrong, we make amends. Barbara wouldn't have had it any other way. About the website--"

"The template is finished, uploaded, and I've transferred everything to Sarah. She knows to call me if there are any problems."

"I know. I want to give you the other half of your

payment." Shushing her protests, he took a check from his jacket pocket. "I've been to your website and the terms are clear: half up front, half on completion of the assignment."

Shanice slipped it into her back pocket. Now she'd be able to better compensate Debra for her help. "Thank you."

They walked out of the hotel into an overcast day. "One last thing," Pastor Robinson said. "Renee has been trying to talk to you. It's important."

Ignoring Renee's calls and voice mail messages felt powerful. Whatever it was – Brandy or something else – Shanice didn't want to get involved. Now Pastor Robinson's involvement had piqued her curiosity.

Shanice got in the car, started it up, but didn't move. She decided to get the call out of the way and end the conversation quickly.

Renee answered on the first ring. "Shanice? I've been trying to reach you forever. You've been avoiding me!"

Shanice tried to keep her voice light. "It's been a rough few weeks. Confronting a killer, avoiding the press, defying my mother's demand that I come back home – I didn't feel like talking. You've got me now. What's up?"

"There's something important that I need to tell you." Renee sounded contrite, a sign that she was about to ask a favor.

"I'm listening."

"It's not going to happen for another seven or eight months, but Walter and I are going to get engaged."

"Excuse me?" Shanice stared at the phone her mouth agape.

"He approached me with the idea. This way, the single women in his congregation can stop competing to be the next Mrs. Robinson. Plus, it will give me some cover too. When a guy offers to lay hands on me, I can evoke my fiancé."

"When is the wedding?" Shanice couldn't believe it, but she didn't know what else to say.

"There's not going to be one. We'll announce our

engagement at church. The story is that we fell in love while helping each other through our grief. By then, I'll be starting the second leg of *A God Man Is Hard to Find* tour. We'll break up in about three or four years."

"How does Brandy feel about this?"

"She hates it, but she understands. Walter and I aren't moving in together. When I'm in town, I'll be doing a lot more solos at Hope Reborn. That's going to be the extent of my involvement; I'm not first lady material."

"Congratulations, I guess?"

"I've assured Walter that I don't have any scandals ready to pop out of the shadows."

Ah, the favor. Renee was asking for her continued silence and distance. Shanice was happy to grant her both. "You're safe on my end. I wish you all the best." Smiling to herself, she put the car in gear. "As far as that congregation is concerned, you better watch your back."

ABOUT THE AUTHOR

Tawanna Sullivan was raised in Baltimore with a solid foundation in the Baptist church and 80s horror movies. Her short stories have been featured in various anthologies, including *Iridescence: Sensuous Shades of Lesbian Erotica*, *Swing! Adventures in Swinging by Today's Top Erotica Writers*, *Dangerous Bargain* and *Forever Vacancy*. Currently living in New Jersey, Tawanna is working on her next mystery and finding new ways to make her wife laugh.

www.ingramcontent.com/pod-product-compliance
Lightning Source LLC
Chambersburg PA
CBHW032120170626
46808CB00006B/2032